PROMISED HEART

A faithful Golden Retriever charts a journey to find the woman who receives her master's heart.

Christopher Dant

SHIRES PRESS
Manchester Center, Vermont

PROMISED HEART

SHIRES PRESS

4869 Main Street, P.O. Box 2200
Manchester Center, VT 05255
www.northshire.com

PROMISED HEART
By Christopher Dant

ISBN 978-1-60571-501-8
First Trade Paperback Edition: July 2020

Printed in the United States of America

To Chauncey, forever

The purple dusk of twilight time

steals across the meadows of my heart

and I am once again with you

Stardust

Lyrics: Mitchell Parish

Music: Hoagy Carmichael

ACKNOWLEDGEMENTS

I am thankful to the many people who have helped me to transform this work from an idea that began nearly two years ago to the novel it has become today.

First, to my wife, Maureen, who provided me with inspiration and many ideas for this story and sat through endless hours of readings and ideas. And to our Golden Retriever, Chauncey, who inspires me every day in many ways. I always looked at her when I got stuck.

The cover of this novel shows Mona Skyrudshaugen and her beautiful Golden Retriever girl Agnes (Dewmist Santolina) from Nord-Odal, Norway. Mona's husband, Allan Tingstveit, who took the remarkable photograph, kindly granted me copyright permission to use it for my cover. It told my story.

For their helpful and insightful reviews, I thank Katie McKenzie, a dog behaviorist and owner of Dog Lover's Training in Vermont as well as Jennifer Jones, owner of a service dog named 'Cooper' and volunteer at Susquehanna Service Dogs. They know dogs well, especially therapy and service dogs, and provided many ideas to help keep my story true.

I also thank Dr. Haddad, a talented and dedicated cardiovascular surgeon at Stanford Medical Center who provided me with background on heart transplantation and treatment. While this is a work of fiction, the idea behind this novel is based in reality. There have been reports in the medical literature that show a person who receives a donor's heart can change in personality. In one study of forty-seven heart transplant patients in Austria, three experienced a distinct change in their personality, taking on the donor's feelings and spirit. They believe, as do I, that the heart is the center of feelings and forms the personality. My story idea first came to me from a beautiful advertisement about becoming an organ donor, an emotional commercial about a man and his dog and how the dog connects with the woman who had received the man's heart.

I also tip my hat to people of Vermont that motivated the creation of some of my characters. My tale was driven by their strength, simplicity, and unspoiled spirit. Characters such as Malcolm Longridge and Sarah Bristoll were inspired by many wonderful Vermonters I have known over the years and the settings were based on Vermont towns I have known. Especially, a place I lived and loved, Thetford, Vermont. Our two-hundred year-old home in Thetford, "Stardust Hill," was the inspiration for Judge Benson's homestead as was the town.

The quotation, the epigraph at the beginning of this novel was taken from the lyrics of the iconic song "Stardust" by Hoagy Carmichael and Mitchell Parish. They reminded me that *I am once again with you*. Like in my novel "Rescue," it's a tribute to my father, Charles "Bud" Dant, a talented and well-known musician and composer now no longer with us. In a small cafe at Indiana University in Bloomington, he wrote the first arrangement of "Stardust" for Hoagy Carmichael, well before Mitchell Parish wrote the beautiful lyrics.

Dad, this is for you, a second time.

This is a work of fiction, but every day, in so many ways, the dogs that I have known throughout my life have inspired me, particularly our own Golden Retriever "Chauncey." Although not a service or therapy dog, she reminds me daily that the bond between man and dog is unwavering and true—one must start with that.

But here, the hand grows shaky. The relationship between man and his dog is ultimately a mystery, really, one that defies words and can only be experienced. Be it on the hunting fields, on the battlefields, or in service, the many ways that dogs help men and women amaze me.

In this novel, I strived to show that beautiful relationship. Tested through time and adversity, that bond is indestructible and unspoiled, and revealed in many different ways.

That unwavering loyalty can be seen in the heartbroken dog lying by his soldier's casket; the dog in the lap of a homeless man, protecting him; the faithful dog waiting every day at the train station for his owner to return, years after the man had died; an old, homeless dog taken in by the kindness of a stranger; the dog at the end of its good life, happy with his final touch.

And in 'Promised Heart,' a heartbroken dog who again finds love with the woman who receives her master's heart.

Dogs are our buddies, our protectors, and ultimately, our saviors.

1

It had been only lately that Chauncey could feel that the house was keeping a secret from her. All throughout the summer and now, into the autumn, she had felt something was going to happen, but no matter where she looked, she couldn't find it. Sometimes when she walked into a room, there was the feeling that the thing that was about to happen had just been right there, just right in front of her, and she would stop and pant and peer around while the feeling seeped away just as mysteriously as it had come to her. Weeks would pass without a sign and then at night it might come again, when, lying nose-to-tail, listening to the murmur of conversation or the clinking of dishes, she would again feel it and she would whisk her tail across the baseboards in long, pensive strokes and silently collect her feet beneath her and wait.

It was a quiet November afternoon, and Chauncey lay in slumber by the sunroom window, her nose sampling the sweet hay gathered in the field behind Judge Benson's house as a cold rain pattered its rhythms against the roof. She knew Dirck was close. Not far away, just in the great room where she had left him only an hour before. She had turned eight a month ago and with advancing age came deeper slumbers in her down time. Her years as a service dog to the veteran had been steady but recently taken on some uncertainty and urgency. Dirck seemed more agitated, less able to cope with his PTSD nightmares, which sharpened her senses and considerable skills, and even in sleep, her radar was alive.

A slight, unexpected noise alerted her. It came from the great room where Dirck had been reading. The sound was quickly followed by a pungent odor. Not the normal acrid smell of fear she knew but something unfamiliar and foul. She quickly gathered and raced through the kitchen and into the great room.

Dirck was slumped onto the arm of the leather couch, his papers scattered to the floor. His eyes were closed. Complex smells flooded her nose. Chauncey leapt to him, pushing against him, licking his face, whining. She pulled back and stared at him for a reaction. It was a familiar sequence for her, waking Dirck up from another PTSD nightmare, another battle dream. But this was not a nightmare. This was unfamiliar and dark. Her master's face was grey, his breathing was shallow, his skin clammy. He tried to speak but his mouth couldn't form words. She put her head to his chest. His heart pounded. Again, she pushed against at him, trying to give him some measure of strength, to wake him. A foul odor pulsed at her in shallow breaths. It smelled like the paint remover he had used for his brushes last summer.

Something had gripped her master but she didn't know what. Or how to help him. She rapidly shifted about on the couch, nudging his face, his arms, crying at him in sharp barks. But he didn't react in a way she remembered. She wasn't prepared for this.

His eyes slowly opened and met hers. He brought his arms around her.

"Chauncey…I can't…breathe girl…."

She pushed her muzzle against his mouth and exhaled, trying somehow, to give him the life that seemed to be leaving him. But it didn't help.

She turned her head and barked, a loud bark. Another. Alert barks. They echoed through the house and beyond. The one close-by neighbor was away, the others too far off to hear her.

Dirck held onto his dog, staring into her sad, unblinking eyes. Memories flooded forward.

It was her unwavering devotion he most remembered. Chauncey had taught him love and friendship, about the beauty of simplicity. He pictured walking with her in the quiet woods, spending the hours together lazily watching the snow fall from the bay window, staring at her soft sleeping face as a shaft of winter sunlight slowly crossed it. She had taught him optimism in the face of adversity, the selflessness acts that kept him safe. This wonderful dog had chosen him as much as he had that day so long ago at Canines Assisting Soldiers, CAS, where her trainer, Dru Vaughn, had dedicated herself to preparing Chauncey for Dirck. For nearly two years, he had walked through his miserable life without his dog's daily assistance and love after she had been stolen. And it was upon her return from that long, uncharted journey that their hearts had become truly one, locked together forever. She had become everything to Dirck, saving him from the nightmares, the suicide attempts, the horrors of addiction, isolation and the crippling fear that came with it. She had first become his service dog six years ago, yet the memories were still clear. But now, they were smothered in dread and the fear of unknown things.

He leaned forward and held Chauncey tightly, his formidable grip giving her some measure of comfort. But he was struggling and uncertain. Another awful minute passed. Dirck sat up and took a deep, indecisive breath.

In the past month, there had been moments of dread. It had been this past summer, not really that long ago, that he began feeling horribly ill. Days of vomiting and high fever, then better, then worse, disorientation and confusion, sleepless nights. But Dirck was strong and each time, he would seemingly return to his normal self. To her, it was just Dirck being sick for a while then back to himself. It was late last August that Dirck's family doctor, Cliff Benford, had told him that his liver was failing, that there was not much that could be done except a liver transplant. But it would have to be in the next months and there were no compatible donors near their Vermont home, nothing even on the East Coast. The years of drinking, the drugs, had caught him. Yet he hadn't touched any for years, at least the years since Chauncey had returned home, but now, there was nothing to be done, just to put his affairs in order. There were not many. Donate his money, dwindled to $85,000, and will his house to CAS and Dru. And then there was Chauncey. Certainly, she would go to Dru, but what would become of her once he was gone? Writing his will had been immensely painful.

He pulled his dog close and lowered his head against her forehead as if to telegraph a message to her. He needed for her to understand some things. He collected and drew a deep breath.

"Chauncey. Listen to me, girl. I can't stay with you much longer. You have given me more than anything in this life. Given me life itself."

Chauncey began licking her lips in fear.

"And I need you to know. To know…in my heart, I always will be with you. I make you this promise. *Always*."

He pulled away and stared at her in silence. Chauncey looked into his glazed eyes. She almost could not recognize the strong and certain face of the man, her master who she given life and that had been hers.

His strong arms slipped away from her and his eyes closed. She began to tremble. Her muzzle shivered and drool dripped to the couch.

She let out a strange noise, not like one of her soft, low moans that Dirck had loved—that relaxed and beautiful sound—but a deep, guttural sound, a horrible wail like the tragic cry of a mother that had just lost its young.

She jumped from the couch and raced frantically about the large room, her head up, crying at the door, to the bay window. Then back to the couch, frantically pushing into Dirck, moving his head with her muzzle, trying again and again to bring him back.

But nothing would wake him to her.

Chauncey stood awkwardly before the lifeless man and threw back her head and bellowed a long, anguished howl, a sound unlike any she had ever made before.

A requiem of grief to the dark and empty room.

2

Dru was late. Very late. She had promised Dirck to be there by noon but part of Route 38 to Glenriver had washed out and the detour was twenty-five miles north around the town of East Rockingham. And it was now late afternoon. She carried Chauncey's updated training papers and new ideas for her therapy training. She was excited to show off her formidable skills to some of the new veterans at CAS.

But mostly she just missed seeing Chauncey. It had been nearly four months since she had last visited Dirck.

But as she pulled into the long, familiar driveway, something was wrong. Usually, when Dirck expected her, they both would appear at the side door and Chauncey would race out to her. That, and there were no lights on and the house was dark.

She opened the car door. That's when she heard the howl.

It was an unusual sound, not like that of a dog. Coyotes were not out this time of year. A long, mournful howl followed by frantic barking.

It was Chauncey!

She ran to the bay window that looked into the great room. The dog was at the window, her paws on the sill, frantically barking, pleading to her. It was dark and she couldn't see Dirck.

She ran to the kitchen door and pulled out her Swiss knife to force the lock loose, a skill from her Marine Corp days.

The door swung open and Chauncey jumped to her, crying, then turned towards the great room and barked frantically.

She knew Dirck was in trouble.

Chauncey ran to the room and jumped to the couch where Dirck lay. Dru switched on the lights.

She grabbed Dirck by the shoulders and shook him forcefully.

"Dirck! Dirck! Can you hear me?"

No response.

She lifted his eyelid. His pupil was dilated. His pulse was weak. She shook again.

"Dirck! Wake up!"

Chauncey was at her side, whining.

She pulled out her phone and punched 9-1-1.

"9-1-1, what's your emergency?"

"Betty, it's Dru. Dru Vaughn. I'm at Dirck's house—3982 Route 44. Need an ambulance immediately! He's in trouble. Now!"

"Dru, thought that was you! Okay, just punched in an alert—they're on their way. What's wrong with him?"

"Don't know, I can't wake him. Still has a pulse but it's weak. Please tell them to hurry."

Billy Hodges had been on the outskirts of Glenriver, gently guiding the ambulance through the streets, testing his new equipment. When the call came in, he had just turned towards Rockingham and was close by.

Billy knew Dirck. He had spent his earlier years at Judge Benson's homestead cutting and staking wood, helping Dirck fix his fences, doing odd jobs. He was a good friend and his heart leapt when he heard Betty's panicked voice.

He slapped his hand across the emergency dials and banked the heavy ambulance into a hard U-turn. The large van screeched along the street, its lights flashing and high-pitched siren screaming as he sped ninety miles an hour through the quiet country streets. They arrived in less than four minutes.

Billy and his senior paramedic placed Dirck on the floor with an oxygen mask. They hooked him to an EKG and began massaging his chest. His eyes remained closed. Billy pulled out his cellphone.

"Response. Is that you Bill?" the hospital dispatcher said.

"Doctor Chamborne, stat! Bill Hodge. We're at Hansen's place in Glenriver. He's unresponsive, shallow breathing, ST-wave irregular, heartrate weak, forty-five beats. Pupils dilated. Skin clammy and yellow!"

Dr. Chamborne, a spry man of seventy-three, was the one cardiologist at the Glenriver Regional Hospital and knew Dirck well. He had even known Dirck's father, Major Douglas G. Hansen. He also knew Cliff Benford, Dirck's family doctor and was aware of the man's health problems. The call didn't surprise him.

"Wrap him, keep him warm, give him pure oxygen, push epinephrine and get him here immediately!" Chamborne ordered.

Dru held tightly onto her shivering dog as the paramedics worked through their orders. Dirck was lifted onto a stretcher and wheeled out to the ambulance. But as the screen door was opened, Chauncey broke free and ran to his side, whining at the lifeless figure on the stretcher before her. Dru her pulled her away. The ambulance doors slammed and Billy signaled to her out the window.

"Stay here. We will call you as soon as Dr. Chamborne knows more about Dirck."

Chauncey shuddered, crying at the ambulance as it disappeared down the dark driveway.

It took a half an hour for Dru to get her back inside.

Gerald Chamborne was at the emergency entrance when the ambulance arrived. His team was prepared for Dirck.

They had to keep him alive. The year after his dog had found her way home, Dirck had become an organ donor. But it wasn't certain which organs would be viable until Dirck was evaluated by the response team.

The stretcher was wheeled into the ER and two physicians began examining Dirck. His breathing and EKG were erratic, his heartbeat slow. They worked quickly.

Dirck lay motionless on the stretcher. In his mind's eye, he was standing alone outside his home. It was dark and cold. In the blackness, he felt a rush of different things. The years of isolation and fear. But the joy of his dog, her deep love. He could feel her head leaning on him, and, as he prepared to leave the earth, an odd comfort washed through him.

A tall grey-haired priest stepped forward. Dirck wasn't baptized Catholic but his father had followed the Church's teachings. He bent over Dirck and signed his forehead with oil.

"Dirck Hansen, peace, courage, and forgiveness unto you. We grant you peace in passing over to the eternal life."

Dirck's face seemed drained of life but he looked calm. He was almost smiling.

The priest looked back to Dr. Chamborne.

"He's ready for God."

The doctors took a final EEG to declare Dirck Hansen brain dead. They wheeled him into the next room.

An hour later, Dru received the phone call. All they could say was that Dirck had passed away peacefully and that she could arrange to have the body transported to the Glenriver Hill Mortuary in another day. The call lasted only twenty seconds. That's all there was. Twenty seconds within a lifetime.

Dirck was only sixty-five.

Dru held onto her shaking dog.

Chauncey's life, all that she ever knew, all that she ever was, was now gone.

3

The realization that Dirck was gone jolted Dru awake. It was 10 p.m. and she had fallen asleep on the floor next to Chauncey. The rain had stopped.

She led her dog to the back sunroom, away from the great room where Dirck had lain only hours before.

She had been through loss with her dog before. She especially remembered when Chauncey was a puppy six months old, and had been separated from her handler Jerry at the prison in her initial "Pups for Prisoners" program. Then there were the two years that she had gone missing and been separated from Dirck. She knew the dog's spirit. It was strong and resilient, but as Dru sat with the despondent dog in her lap that dark evening, she wasn't sure what might happen to her spirit, and her own grief made it all the worse.

In the morning, she would take Chauncey back to CAS in upstate New York, over two hours away. It was a place her dog knew well, her second home, a place she would be safe and cared for. She would call her staff to make the arrangements tomorrow. But tonight, they would both have to find some peace here in the dark and empty house.

In the middle of the awful night, Chauncey jumped from Dru, and ran into the great room. She jumped to the couch, desperately pushing into the spot where Dirck had lain.

To her, his scent and the memory of him were one. He was gone, but he still clung on the old leather couch. She deeply ached to feel him again and pressed her face, her ruff into the cushions, trying to sense his hand, feel the heat of his body through his shirt. She jumped down and followed her nose up the stairs into his bedroom where, night after night for as long as she could remember, she would lay in silence at his bedside, listening to him breathe. Every night, she would lie at his feet, eager and alert, watching his face, dwelling upon it, studying it, memorizing his many features. She would follow his every expression, each nuance of his features, his movements, his sounds, his smells. They were all drawn up inside her.

She ran back downstairs to wake Dru, begging to go out.

Chauncey ran madly out into the darkness of her familiar yard. It was the middle of the night and the remnants of light from a waxing moon faintly lit the landscape. She looked up at the dark shafts of the firs and birch along driveway. They were silhouettes against a grey sky, the night winds slowly bending their charcoaled skeletons against one another. Through the interlacing boughs of weeping willows, faint whispers called their sad sounds forward.

She went to the stone wall where she had last buried a bone that Dirck had bought her on the first day she had lived here. She had kept it there for years. He would dig it up every now and again and she would bury it again and again, remembering that he would wrestle it from her in jest, only to let her bury it once more. She found its bony edge and pulled it free, taking bone and dirt and worms into her mouth, searching for his smell, just some trace of him. And, once she saw its futility, she ran out further into the yard, hoping to hear him clogging after her, his breath following closely behind, and she stopped and turned, hoping he would suddenly appear, silent and gestureless, beside her.

For she was not without her own selfish desires—to try and hold her life motionless and constant, to measure herself against that, to know she was alive just because he didn't acknowledge her in passing. That constancy might prevail if she attended her world carefully. But all of it was folly, for now, there was no constancy, only those things that sapped her, undefined her, and she felt diminished. In her life until now, she had been nourished and sustained by Dirck but now she couldn't assign him an identity outside her own world. It was her sense of being alive that was now thinned by the lack of his spirit devoted to her.

She ran to the garage where his car had been parked now for several days and she lay next to it in the cold darkness, hoping for a faint sent, some newly discovered object, some simple revelation of him. His car was enough to calm her for a short time. And when Dru went out after her, she brought one of Dirck's shirts and lay it next to her, if only to further ease her unending burden.

Chauncey led Dru into the back field along the stone fence where the fragments of time had been snagged and hung only for her to know. She stopped at a stand of young ash trees, one of which still contained the sharp burr from a branch where Dirck had cut his hand long ago. His scent was still there, faint but still pungent and sweet. She sat next to it, her nose pointing down to the ragged edge. Her eyes rose slowly up to Dru. They were large and dark like that of a young dog who had lost its way home. It was a look she had seen only once before when Chauncey had been taken from the prison training program. Defeated, heartbroken. It had taken months of training to bring her confidence back from that defeat, but this time, she feared the lost dog before her might never again regain herself.

It was after 3 a.m. before Dru could coax her back into the house. She lit a fire and held Chauncey closely as they lay on the floor of the great room, watching the flames flicker against the darkness.

There was no sleep that night, only the sound of silence.

The next day, Dru arranged for some of Dirck's friends to help close the up house. Inside his safe, she read the signed will giving Dru and CAS the $85,000 in cash. And the deed to the home, the Judge Benson's homestead. The last page was the paper deciding on arrangements for Chauncey. Over the past years, Dirck had repeatedly told her that she was to take his dog back to CAS if anything were to happen to him.

As Chauncey lay in her lap, she re-read the simple unemotional sentence.

Upon my death, I, Dirck Hansen, entrust the care of my service dog Chauncey, to Dru Vaughn at Canine Assisting Soldiers in New York.

Later that week, Dirck's funeral was held at the Glenriver *All Saint's Church.* Dru and Dave brought Chauncey. Several of Dirck's veteran friends attended, many of whom had helped him during the long months when his dog had gone missing years earlier. Even Jake Tollinger and his daughter Joanne attended, sitting in the front row. It had been Jake—the man who had originally stolen the dog—who had been transformed by Dirck's forgiveness. And he struggled the most with his fellow veteran's death.

Dru held Chauncey by her halter as she pulled and cried to get at Dirck's casket.

Even the strongest of men in the small church wept.

They gathered in the snowy graveyard for a final goodbye. A photograph of Dirck with Chauncey was passed around. It showed Dirck standing in his Army dress uniform with his new service dog sitting by his side, the photograph that Dave Ballard had taken on the day Dirck had brought his new service dog home. It was a sweet photograph, full of new life and promise.

Some had memories to share. One veteran recounted how Dirck had helped him face suicide, another told stories of the agonizing hours after Chauncey had gone missing those many years ago. Jake Tollinger, even, offered a simple prayer to the man, a prayer to service and sacrifice, and to the dog who had given Dirck everything.

The minister placed the photograph and Dirck's service cap upon the casket.

Chauncey watched as it was slowly lowered into the grave.

It was a simple wooden box, man-made, no more like Dirck than the trees of the forest she had shared with him.

4

Shannon had just finished dinner when her phone rang. It was Sunday night and she wasn't expecting calls. She listened blankly to the tinny recording as she stacked plates.

"This is Shannon. Please leave me a message," her gravelly voice announced.

"Miss Murphy, this is UNOS. Please call us back at 1-800-833-3983 as soon as you get this message. It's urgent," a woman said.

She lunged for the phone. Dishes cascaded to the floor.

Shannon Marie Murphy was a forty-five-year-old unmarried woman who lived alone in her two-bedroom apartment in East Cabot, a small northern-belt Vermont town that had once been a center of the northeast trades, full of opportunity with a lively, growing community. Wool and timber had been plentiful, and the rivers ran fast, turning mill wheels in the small thriving town. Community-based factories produced croquet sets, hockey sticks, rakes, ax handles, wooden toys for young children. Mill-centered towns like East Cabot peppered the green mountains until the turn of the twentieth century, when changes in transportation and manufacturing closed many of them, leveling industrial communities. At its peak, the East Cabot mill had one hundred men working and twenty teams of horses. Amidst the struggle to keep going, the floods came. First in 1927 when months of unceasing rainfall and rising waters flooded the town, nearly wiping East Cabot from the map. Yet it rose back for almost seven years until late 1934, when a hurricane hit the East coast and swept into Vermont, driving out the remaining families. Its restoration was long and difficult with the steep landscape and dampened spirits. But it again survived and the few Vermonters that remained to rebuild were resilient and tough, always believing in another future for East Cabot.

And that included Shannon Murphy.

Every day for the past several years, she had walked the four long blocks along the shuttered factories and hollowed-out downtown, through the haunting dark images of a vanished industrial luster, making her way to the small, refurbished brick building with its inconspicuous sign that read *The Caledonian Record.* The *Record* was a distinctly edgy newspaper that served the people of Cabot County.

It was a good place to write. There was no lack of stories about the forgotten factory workers, torn-apart families, suicides, rising opiate deaths. But, too, there were many hopeful narratives of redemption amidst the rubble of life, of resilience against impossible odds. It was real, exhilarating and stirring, yet heartbreaking and depressing.

Back at the beginning, fifteen years earlier, Shannon's talent for writing had been noticed, quite serendipitously, by Caledonian's editor, Bud Travis, an East Cabot native. At the time, Bud's chief editor of many years, Johnny Murray, had written a lengthy op-ed about East Cabot's rise and demise, a piece he had spent months crafting, an editorial he felt defined his long writing career. Not long after it appeared in print, Bud had received an anonymous letter along with Murray's piece generously marked up in red. The simple two-page letter had taken Shannon just a half hour to write. In part, it read:

Death of an American Small Town.
Mr. Murray's attempted character 'sketch,' if you might call it that, of East Cabot's demise and rise, delivers us hopeful readers with merely a glancing blow, a poorly crafted mischaracterization of East Cabot's true history—a history ripe with hopeful industrial transformations of a rural character seen by the town's beloved Martha Stanford's Curiosities and John Munger's Mill Socks and Jumpers, by Gerald and Mildred Jilly's Curiosities, the generations of them all, flattened out by idle muddy boots that had once passed to struggling factories behind town streets where love had lived. Yet in small ways in many small rooms, love lives and remains here, here in our East Cabot, Vermont.

It went on, double spaced and typed in Courier font, with its one typo neatly hand-corrected in red. There were stories of the townsfolk and the families that Shannon knew, stories of tragic demise with industrial rollovers. It was dense and deep, but simple and true. It made Bud Travis cry. It was signed "Anon."

The following day, a letter from the editor appeared in the *Caledonian Record* asking for the writer of "the brilliantly written letter" to come forward.

Shannon obliged.

After all, what did she have to lose? She was new in East Cabot back then, having moved there only two months earlier to live with her younger sister, Brigid. They had moved from Burrs Oaks, just 100 miles north, another rural Vermont town where they had been born and raised. Shannon had attended Burrs Oaks High School, was educated at Vermont College just 50 miles from her home, and settled back in Burrs Oaks with a handsome local carpenter and horseman, Paulson, a man she adored. But Shannon didn't know how to show affection, for him or anyone else really, and after only a year, Paulson left her for someone who could, someone he later married. It crippled her emotionally.

Back then, Shannon had been only thirty years old and was lonely. She had moved back into her childhood home to live with her mother, Mrs. Mary Murphy, a widow for ten years who, at only fifty-eight years of age, had been incapacitated by heart failure. Through the constant grey depression of her mother's ongoing disease and the heartache of losing Paulson, she pressed quietly on with her work in the trades, writing instructions for assemblymen in the fading Burrs Oaks Woolen Mill, a job that ended when the mill closed the month before her mother's death. Mary left her daughter the little money she had, $3,000 after legal fees, but nothing else except for a few moth-eaten wool sweaters and skirts that didn't fit her.

The move to East Cabot had lifted Shannon's spirits. It was shortly after the move that she had had typed the letter to the editor on Brigid's Oliver personal typewriter, which had been gifted to Brigid by her then-boyfriend.

A week later, Bud Travis hired Shannon as his chief editor and demoted Johnny to her editorial assistant.

Her first stories drew immediate notice by other small local newspapers—*The Buford News*, *Herford Herald*—and after a year, she began receiving calls from editors at *The New York Times* and *The Washington Post.* Her brilliant pieces were reprinted in the prestigious *Yankee Magazine* and *The Atlantic.*

Yet she always thought her writing was pedestrian, perhaps at best just simple and direct. There was a brilliance to its simplicity and emotion she never saw. She just wanted to tell real stories of the people who lived here, many of them her friends, and she strove to show her readers their characters, their lives and loves. And their miseries. Shannon's stories made her readers cry and laugh, and the paper would receive letters each week asking more about the people she wrote about, their families, what became of them, how to get in touch with them, some wanting to donate to them. The families of East Cabot found unexpected hope in Shannon's stores and she became their heroine.

Despite the recognition, she kept a low profile, living quietly and simply with her sister Brigid in the small rented second-floor apartment on Danville Hill Road. She was visited infrequently by the one or two friends she had made from the paper. With Brigid gone much of the time to visit her boyfriend, she was left alone to write. She enjoyed the solitude.

But it was in that last year alone that Shannon had begun to notice the changes.

First, climbing the apartment stairs became more difficult and she was breathless just walking around the apartment. She woke every morning with deep and persistent cough. She largely dismissed this all as getting older. But then, the physical manifestations began to appear. Much of the time, her legs and ankles remained swollen and she began coughing up pink mucus. She didn't move around much and over a year, her weight shot up to over one hundred sixty, which on her five-two, normally slender frame was considerable, and yet her appetite was low.

Then, her mind began to falter. She couldn't concentrate on her writing and was easily distracted. Often, she would forget what she had written or even if she needed to write. She lost her house keys, her purse, didn't remember whether or not she had gone shopping. She slept only three hours a night.

And one day, Brigid called but Shannon couldn't recognize her and hung up.

She didn't go into work for fear of having to climb stairs and walk the long blocks to work. At that point, she had been at the *Caledonian Record* for nearly sixteen years and her absence concerned Bud.

He went to visited her. She didn't look good and he phoned Alex Mills, a recently retired East Cabot cardiologist.

Dr. Mills was shocked by the woman's appearance. Her face was puffy and her eyes swollen. She was bloated and couldn't move well. She looked like a woman in her late seventies instead of just forty-eight.

"Shannon, Bud asked me to come see you. I understand you're having some difficulty walking and breathing. How long has this been going on?" Alex Mills said.

"About a year. Maybe two now. Can't remember. I've been coughing up this pink foamy stuff in the morning. Can't climb stairs anymore."

The doctor raised her pantlegs. Her legs and ankles were swollen and pink. He listened to her heart. The symptoms were clear.

"Shannon, your coughing, erratic heartbeat, the swelling. It all points to chronic heart failure. Did your family have this problem?"

"Mom did. She died some years ago, back when she was about my age," she said but then suddenly realized her mother was not even six years older than she was now when she suddenly died from heart failure.

Her brow wrinkled and she looked down.

"Am I going to…? How much time do I have?"

Alex Mills had been in practice for over twenty-five years but had never seen a patient this advanced.

"We need to get you into the hospital and run some tests to know more. For now, I'm going to get you some pills—they're called beta blockers—they will help your heart and make you feel better so you can get around. We'll get Patricia Tatters to check you. She's a brilliant cardiologist from the Cleveland Clinic. She'll help you through this," he said.

While Alex Mills stayed with Shannon, Bud got her a bottle of white pills from the local pharmacy and that week, they secured her a first-floor apartment.

By the following week, the pills dropped her blood pressure and reduced her heart fluttering. Her swelling went down and she began to move about more easily. She returned to work and began to feel more like her old self, wise-cracking with her co-workers, writing sharply and brilliantly.

But her hope was short lived.

Later that month, Shannon spent a day at the Alstead General Hospital in Rockingham, not far from her home. Dr. Tatters and two other cardiologists reviewed her chest x rays, ECG, stress test, her MRI images, and blood tests. All pointed to chronic heart failure. Class IV failure. Advanced.

They agreed that repairing blood vessels and clearing out any plaque or even giving replacing heart valves wouldn't help in the long run.

Shannon remained at the hospital for two more days to receive stronger heart therapies—cardiac resynchronization, defibrillator therapies, infusions of cardiac receptor blockers. On the third day, Dr. Tatters and her team visited her.

"Shannon, these are my colleagues. Dr. Christopher Davis, a senior cardiologist from Dana Farber in Boston, Dr. Burke, our new cardiologist resident, and Dr. Tenvers, who worked with me at Cleveland Clinic. You've been stabilized for now. Your swelling has decreased and your pressure is down to normal. But it's temporary. Your heart has been damaged and it's unable to pump normally to keep you going. It's only going to get worse."

"Worse? How? When?"

"You need a new heart. Our only recourse is to place you into our transplant recipient program. It's not certain when…"

Shannon interrupted her.

"Am I going to die?"

She was sitting up in bed, shaking.

"We're going to do everything we can to keep you healthy, but there's no certainty when we'll find a suitable donor heart. We'll first need to take some social and psychological evaluations, blood and tissue tests. We can start that today, if you agree. Shannon, do you want a new heart?"

The question surprised her. Why would she not?

"I have no choice unless I want to die, is that what you're saying?"

"Yes. We can keep you comfortable, but your heart will eventually give out. With these medicines, you might be able to get by for another half year or more, but probably not much longer. I'm sorry."

But the doctor saying she was sorry didn't help. It sounded almost unprofessional. The other three cardiologists left, leaving Shannon alone with Patricia Tatters.

Shannon stared down at her hands, which had yellowed from the IV lines and medications. Her skin looked old and wrinkled. There was a long silence. She looked up.

"I don't want to die. I want to live! Please. I need to live!"

She began crying.

The doctor sat on the bed and took her hand.

"I promise you, Shannon, I will do everything I can to keep you alive. We'll get you a new heart."

That afternoon, a team of nurses, social workers, psychologists, and more doctors went through Shannon's history. Her family support, finances, mental health, her living situation, all evaluations the transplant team needed to approve her as a heart recipient.

She was sent home with four new medications and instructions for a new diet and exercises. She had discussed it all with Brigid, who moved back in with her sister from the boyfriend's place nearby. She was told there would be trips to and from the hospital in Boston three hours away, overnight stays, weeks, maybe months, of rehabilitation at home, repeat visits to the hospital, a special diet that she would need to prepare.

Yet Brigid never saw it as a sacrifice. When she was still very young, Brigid had been through two miserable breakups, got hooked on opiates when she had turned seventeen, and trudged through drug rehab and a serious depression for a long year. Through it all, Shannon pulled Brigid out of what looked like the end for her back in Burrs Oaks, even as she was walking through her own miserable life without her love Paulson and having to take care of their dying mother.

They had been back home a week when the call came.

She dove for the phone.

"Is this Shannon? Shannon Marie Murphy?" a woman said.

"Yes, yes, who is this?"

She was out of breath.

"My name is Nancy Batton. I am a senior transplantation nurse from the Alstead General Hospital in Rockingham. I am calling for Dr. Patricia Tatters, your cardiologist. You have been approved for the transplant program."

"Approved? Are you sure?"

She was shaking.

"We received the go-ahead today and your name was placed into the United Network for Organ Sharing, UNOS, a nationwide secured database for transplant organ recipients and donors. As soon as a match is identified, UNOS will contact you. Is this phone number the best way to reach you, Ms. Murphy?"

"Yes! Please let me know how to reach you or UNOS."

Phone numbers were exchanged. Shannon did not use a computer or even have a smartphone. The landline was her only link to a new heart.

It was frightening.

That night, the sisters sat together on the couch talking about how the new heart would make Shannon feel, what she would do after she got it. Whether it would change her. Would it come from a man or woman? How had the heart donor lived and died?

"I'm not going to change anything, Brig'. Stayin' right here in East Cabot and continue writing for the *Record.* Bud is going to keep me going, giving me time off for this. It's what I want to do. Nothing changes."

"Yes, but what if the new heart changes who you are. What if…." Brigid choked up.

"I'm not going to change, silly. I will still be me. You and I will always be together after this."

But Shannon remembered what one of the psychologists had told her. Thirty years ago, there had been the report of a women who had taken on the personality and feelings of her heart donor.

In essence, becoming her donor.

5

Shannon was on the floor amidst broken dishes struggling with the phone receiver. She caught her breath.

"Yes…this is Shannon!"

"This is Michaela Turner of UNOS, the United Network…."

"Yes, yes, I know who UNOS is. This is Shannon!"

"Miss Murphy, can you confirm your birthdate for me?"

"April 12, 1968."

"We are calling you to let you know we have identified a heart donor for you. A match."

There was silence on the line.

"Are you still with me, Miss Murphy?"

"Yes! Are you sure? When? Who?"

"The donor heart was confirmed by Nancy Batton, the senior transplantation nurse from the Alstead General Hospital in Rockingham. She works for Dr. Patricia Tatters. You will need to make immediate arrangements to come down to Massachusetts General Hospital, where the transplant procedure will take place. Will you have a family member help make your arrangements?"

"Oh, yes, yes. My sister will take me there and stay through the surgery."

"Fine. A coordinator from Massachusetts General Hospital will phone you within the hour to give you the information for your surgery."

Her old heart began to flutter. She fell back to the floor. The call had come only a month after Shannon had been approved for the new heart. Now she had one!

Brigid walked in to find her sister on the floor, the phone still in her hand. She was sobbing.

"They have a heart for me!" she gasped. "A new heart! I'm going to live!"

That afternoon was filled with phone calls to her doctor, transplant coordinators at Massachusetts General Hospital, talks with Bud at the *Record*, hotel arrangements in the city of Foxborough near the hospital. The surgery would take most of one day and rehabilitation a week before she could return home.

"God, can you believe it? I'm getting new heart!"

She was anxious but delirious. And most of all, grateful that she would get another chance at life. It had been years of chest pain, fatigue, depression. But most of all, not knowing. Now she knew.

They sat cross-legged on the couch facing each other.

"God, Brig' I wonder whose heart I'll get. They wouldn't tell me. It wasn't part of the donor's wishes. Maybe another woman? I wonder…."

"I don't think it matters Shan'. They wouldn't have matched it unless it was okay."

"I know that, but whose…I mean where will the heart come from? How had they lived…what had they done…how they died?"

The following day, Brigid drove Shannon to Foxborough and checked her into the cardiac unit at Massachusetts General Hospital. It was early December, a time when people stayed inside but here, the cold season halted nothing. The hospital was a huge six-story facility teeming with traffic and people.

Within two hours, Shannon was resting in a bed crammed with instruments and monitors. The transplant coordinator and surgeon walked in.

"Hello Miss Murphy. I'm Dr. Daniel Pratt and this is Michelle Kerr, our transplant coordinator. I will be the lead doctor putting in your new heart along with our cardiologist Dr. Christopher Davis and his team. Your surgery will be about four hours. You'll be placed on a heart-lung machine to keep blood circulating through your body while we remove your old heart, and attached your new donor heart with all the correct plumbing."

The doctor stood close to the bed's edge, his hand on Shannon's arm as he described the procedure. The doctor didn't appear old, although in his face was written the memory of many things both glad and sorrowful. He looked kind. And competent.

She smiled.

"Thank you, doctor. I guess my heart just kind of pooped out, huh?" she said but immediately wished she hadn't tried to make light of such a heavy decision.

The doctor stepped back and laughed.

"Yes, Shannon. It 'pooped' out for sure. But we've got a good strong heart for you, so no worries. You'll be back in the game before too long. Once you're all done here, Dr. Christopher Davis will look after your long-term care."

The conversation became more serious when the transplant coordinator listed the possible complications. Bleeding, infection, blood clots, heart attack, stroke.

And rejection.

She sat up and looked at the woman.

"Rejection?"

"Yes, there is the possibility of heart rejection. This happens rarely in transplantations and we have ways of treating that. Very small chance in your case. Your donor heart is quite compatible."

"Compatible? How?"

"The donors tissue type and blood type and size were a strong match."

Shannon thought she had meant a compatible personality.

"What happens if the heart changes how I feel or think or…."

The woman's brow furled.

"That's unlikely to happen. You'll be healthy again, that's the main thing," she said, clearly skirting the question.

The procedure would be the following day at one o'clock. Shannon would eat a small dinner and then nothing the next day.

It wasn't until early the next evening when Brigid's cellphone finally buzzed. She had not eaten dinner.

"Brigid Murphy, this is Marie, your sister's transplant nurse. Your sister is out of surgery and in intensive care. Everything went just fine. You'll be able to see her first thing tomorrow morning after she's fully awake. Nothing to worry about on your end, just enjoy your evening and we'll give you a call when you can come see her."

Brigid was elated. But apprehensive.

Yes, but what if the new heart changes who you are? she had remembered saying to her sister. The experts had told her that wouldn't happen but she worried her sister wouldn't be the same.

The next morning, as Brigid turned the corner into Shannon's hospital room, she wasn't prepared for what she saw.

Her sister was sitting up in bed, smiling. Her face was flushed, complementing her red hair. Her piercing blue eyes were bight and alive. She looked like the Shannon of ten years ago.

To Brigid's relief, her sister immediately recognized her.

"Brig'! I'm done! Can you believe it? They said it took almost five hours. Wow!" She flashed a large grin.

Brigid stared at her. She reached out to touch her but stopped short, afraid of disturbing the tubes twisted about her. The bandages on her chest were impressive.

"Shan' you look…so good! Your color is back!"

For what seemed like years, Shannon's skin had been pale, almost yellow in spots and her face was unnaturally wrinkled. The woman before her looked twenty years younger.

"Yeah, they let me look in the mirror. I have oxygen to my body! So much energy all of a sudden!"

Daniel Pratt and his young intern walked in.

"Hello Shannon. How are you feeling this morning?"

"Doctor! So good to see your face again! I'm feeling great. I'm breathing so much better."

"Yes, that happens after the new heart. Let me have a listen."

The room was silent as the doctor listened. He pulled back and wrapped the stethoscope around his neck.

"Your new heart sounds really good. Strong!"

Shannon stared at him through tears.

"I know how it feels from my patients. I am happy that you have a new strong heart. We just want to make sure it stays healthy to keep you healthy. We'll know a lot more in the next day or two."

After another half hour of visits, Shannon was alone for the first time.

In the quiet of the room, she could feel the heart beating within her, filling her with life.

But she didn't know the secrets it held.

6

Dave Ballard was outside CAS waiting for Dru. It was late and all dogs were asleep in the kennels. It was cold, much colder than usual for December, but the cold wasn't on his mind. Dave had been Chauncey's main trainer back when she had gone through service training, and he had known Dirck Hansen well.

The trip from Judge Benson's homestead had taken a long three hours. Dru climbed out of her car and looked at Dave, her eyes dark and heavy. Dave held her while she wept.

Chauncey was sitting in the van's front seat, staring out to the field, a familiar sight from her younger years. CAS was where she had grown up, the place she had become a service dog. Back then, it had been a bright happy place with sweet memories. But as she stared out to the familiar field, it looked dark and unhappy. It reminded her only of Dirck.

"It took us a long while, Dave. I had to stop every hour and just hold onto Chauncey to let her know she was okay. Half way through, I brought her up front and held onto her while I drove. She's in a bad way. I'm not sure how she'll handle this."

"We'll find a way, Dru. Chauncey's a strong girl. I remember her coming out of that funk after her prison program. She'll…."

"Oh, this is so much worse. She's lost Dirck and he was everything to her. Remember Mike Jefferies, that vet who had passed away after having Bella for all those years? She never recovered from his death. She carried that sorrow with her to her final days. I just don't know about Chauncey."

"This is the best place for her now. We'll get her back. You have a great staff that knows how to handle anything. We'll find a way to lead her through this."

But as she led Chauncey from the front seat, his reassurance didn't help her. Dave bent down to greet her but she just walked past him towards the field and stared blankly out.

This the place had first seen Dirck, the man she would entrust her life to. His face appeared in the dark about her. She remembered him saying *I love you, pretty girl…kiss!* She remembered diving towards him for a big sloppy kiss, making him fall backward as they lay together in the grass.

That was so long ago. Sadness swept through her.

Dru fastened her lead, but Chauncey wouldn't budge. She had found some small solace here in the dark field, it seemed. They both sat with her for another hour in the cold before she decided to turn back.

Chauncey lay next to Dru's bunk in her facility but throughout the long, unsettled night, she remained awake. This place, its smells, her early memories, all stirred in her.

The next morning, Sharon Farnum, CAS's veterinarian was brought in. Chauncey sat in the corner of small room looking aimlessly around as Farnum checked her vitals, drew some blood, took a urine sample.

Sharon remembered the last time she had seen the dog. She had been barely three years old and she recalled how the young dog wiggled about uncontrollably, trying to lick her face and mouth her hand, squealing with exuberance at every turn.

But the dog before her appeared defeated. She didn't return Sharon's gaze and her eyes were watery and dull. Gone was the smile, the bright eyes, the excitement. Her tail was tucked between her legs. Chauncey's head hung and she drooled.

She looked more like a dog of thirteen years.

"I don't remember Chauncey ever looking this bad, Dru. Her reflexes are off and she's unresponsive. I'll let you know more when we get back her tests. But in the meantime, stay close to her and make sure she drinks and eats. And get her outside for some diversion."

"I will, Sharon. But I'm worried. Such a broken little heart."

CAS sat on the outskirts of the small New York town of Baker's Mills near the Siamese Ponds, stunningly beautiful lakes within a hilly, wooded country. It was mid-December but only two months earlier, the place had been teeming with tourists hiking and motoring through the vast countryside filled with vermilion maples and pale-yellow poplars, and here and there, splashed scarlet clusters of deep red berries against the dark green canopy of spruce and cedar. Now, the evergreens were dominant, punctuating the stark white hills and empty camps. It was a place Chauncey had grown up, her first taste with nature. She had happily roamed these hills and valleys and small back roads. This was her other home, thick with memories of youth and first loves.

That winter morning, things were quiet at CAS except for the occasional bright barks of happy dogs. Dave and Dru met with the other trainers and decided that Chauncey needed to interact with other dogs.

They led Chauncey out to meet two handsome dogs, a Golden named "Tucker" and a black mix "Roo." Both looked up at the new dog. They approached Chauncey, their tails swinging and heads cocked in anticipation of play. But she turned from them and walked to the other side of the yard. As they approached her rear, she spun about and erupted in threatening barks. Dru led the dogs away. She had never seen her dog display such aggression. She took Chauncey back to the room where she curled back onto bed for the rest of the day.

Two weeks past. Dru and her team had no success in getting Chauncey to play with other dogs. She wouldn't respond to any of the trainers who tried to lead her through even basic commands. She ate only once a day.

By the end of the second week, Dr. Farnum returned with test results.

"Her vitals are okay. Her glucose and blood cell tests were normal as were her digestive and endocrine tests. Her urine shows she's not hydrated and we need to get fluids in her. But one test was odd."

"Odd? What?"

"One protein was abnormally high—it's called beta temerulase. It's an enzyme in the blood. It's not usually tested but they spotted abnormalities in her immune panel and we tested further. That protein points to 'hyperosmia'—that's a fancy term for an acute sense of smell. Most dogs detect scents thirty feet underground or even week-old human fingerprints, but a dog with hyperosmia goes way beyond that," said Sharon.

"Wonder what caused that?"

"It's a change sometimes associated with loss or trauma. The turbinates—those complex folds deep in the nose contain scent-detecting cells—greatly increase in sensitivity. Technically, we call those the *vomeronasal organ*—the sac on the roof of a dog's mouth and nose, more commonly called *Jacobson's organ*. It's where the serious business of smells gets translated to the brain."

"And Chauncey has this increased sensitivity to smell?"

"Yes, apparently. There're so few examples, but one dog I knew about was able to locate a person lost at sea for a month, many miles away. Dogs with hyperosmia even react to whales beneath the sea. It's really rare."

"Well our first thing is to get her hydrated and some food in her. Back to a basic health."

"Sure, Dru, we'll set up an IV for fluids and we can feed her some high-protein liver, a taste she seems to like. I'll stick around the rest of the day and help you."

"But this…hyperosmia…is there a way we can test for that to be sure?"

"Yes, there's a standard test called 'Decreasing Thresholds Field Test' or 'DTF.' We take a known scent, like the liver treats she loves, and bury them in smaller amounts at increasing distances from the dog. There a threshold at which a normal dog cannot detect it—that's usually a small amount of a scent buried up to two miles away in an open field like you have out back."

"Let's set it up once she's healthy and more responsive. I need to get her out onto the trails and exercise her. I'm spending a lot of time with her to let her know she's not alone."

"Yes, that's good. She's spent the last many years following Dirck and getting all her stimulus from him. She had a big job to do with him. She doesn't have that anymore. You need to replace that, give her a new job."

"That's what I thought. I have to replace Dirck. I'm thinking she would be a great therapy dog."

"I'll help in any way I can."

Dru fed Chauncey freshly cooked liver, beef, and vegetables by hand each morning and evening. The stimulus of Dru's smell and kind hand calmed the dejected dog and she began regaining strength and confidence. After two courses of IV fluids, she could tell her dog felt better. And by another week, she was able to take long walks and began responding to other dogs.

By mid-January, Sharon Farnum returned along with a veterinary tech for the DTF test, which took place in the ten-acre field behind CAS. The techs buried a gram of liver just below the ground a thousand feet out. Chauncey immediately found it. Then, a half gram another thousand feet out. Immediately found. This followed the normal decreasing threshold of half a gram a mile out. Found.

"Normally, dogs couldn't have found that. So, now, we'll take quarter gram of liver and bury it at the two-mile mark," Sharon said. "No dog can detect that, not even a bloodhound."

They buried the tiny sliver of food and let it sit overnight. The next morning, Dru led Chauncey to the field and donned her electronic collar, allowing her to track her dog's movement.

"Find!" she commanded.

Chauncey raced into the snow-bound field, nearly disappearing except for faint flashes of snow. They watched the monitor. The blinking dot was headed directly for the buried treat.

Chauncey dug into the snow and dirt to find the tiny buried liver. Two miles out.

They buzzed her back. Chauncey proudly smiled up at them.

"My God, there wasn't even a hunt for it. She found it immediately!" Sharon said to her tech. "That's amazing! She definitely has hyperosmia."

"What's that mean for her?" Dru said.

"Not sure. But her nose will be flooded with many smells, some very far away. It could confuse her."

They led her back and sat with her inside the facility, praising her for her great job. Sharon placed her hands on her muzzle. Suddenly, Chauncey pointed her nose to Dr. Farnum's chest and sniffed intently. She looked up and barked.

"My God, Dru! She must detect that small tumor the doctors had found in my right breast a year ago. It was removed. I hope it's not grown back."

"Maybe it's a perfume or cream?" said Dru.

But Sharon Farnum knew Chauncey had detected something inside her.

While Chauncey had become more responsive, Dru could still tell she still lacked attention. She remembered the simple commands—down, shake, sit, fetch objects—yet the dog had lost that spark trainers had remembered. She remained oddly detached.

Dru had to try something different. She called in Dave.

"Dave. I'm think of bringing back Callie. She's been on a three-month stint with the Glenview Cove Hospital. They were so close. It could help her."

Callie was a handsome black Labrador Retriever that Dru had brought to CAS years earlier to train as a therapy dog. She had been barely four years old when the two dogs had first met. It had been Chauncey who, on the run from her captors' years earlier, rescued Callie from captivity, saving her from certain death, and guided her through miles of forests on her journey home.

Callie had come to learn how her companion had trained to help Dirck and she became close to the veteran in the years before his death. She had grown into an impressive Labrador who became Chauncey's steady companion and protector until Dru had brought her to CAS. Callie had been at the facility for over three years now and had become one of her most sought-after therapy dogs. She was a natural with just the right touch, knowing when to come close, when to remain apart.

"Yes, let's bring her back. It'll help Chauncey."

They made the arrangements and within two days, Callie returned to CAS.

The following day, Dru led Chauncey to the back facility. Like the times before, she returned to the far corner of the enclosure, staring out to the familiar field.

Dave led Callie into the yard and made her sit. Callie spotted her companion and shivered with excitement. Dave unleashed her and she sprang forward but suddenly stopped short. She sensed something was wrong and let out a sharp bark. A familiar bark. Chauncey turned. For a moment, both dogs stood frozen in the snow-covered yard staring at one another.

Callie's scent bolted Chauncey into recognition and she raced to her. Their muzzles met and Chauncey's furry tail opened and swung wildly.

In the frozen morning air, the dogs danced about one another, licking each other's muzzles.

"Oh, Dave, she remembers!"

"This is a good sign. This will really help."

They left the dogs play but by afternoon, they were brought inside to a shared pen. Bright barks erupted when Dru returned with their dinner.

"Oh, you two cute girls…you both hungry?"

Chauncey barked and looked up at her. Her bright eyes flashed with that happy look Dru remembered from years earlier.

She set down bowls. The dogs ate ravenously, growling amicably at each other as they feasted on the rich meal, their metal bowls shifting along the cement floor. Dru smiled.

"You girls were hungry! How about an after-meal treat?"

She reached in her apron and produced small liver chunks. The dogs leapt to her, pleading for the treats.

They were inseparable.

But their reunion would be short-lived.

7

It was just before Valentine's day when the sisters returned to East Cabot from nearly ten weeks at the Massachusetts hospital. Shannon had been one of Dr. Pratt's best patients with no complications, perfect blood tests, no infections.

Your new heart seems to like you, Shannon he had told her.

The cardiac unit had been her second home for nearly three weeks, the place she had been given life. On her last day, the hospital corridors were filled with colored balloons and bouquets of flowers along the row of nurses and doctors. Shannon and Brigid walked proudly along them as they left the hospital.

Everything was easy for her now. Walking down the hospital corridors, up the stars, getting in and out of Brigid's station wagon. Gone was the dizziness, the edema and bloating, and constant headaches. And the crippling fear. She had lost twenty-five pounds. Her puffy face was sculped and her eyes were now bright.

As they crossed onto Vermont Route 100A, East Cabot came into view. Shannon almost didn't recognize her hometown. It looked new and brilliant. Along the run-down factories and the neglected, peeling Victorian homes lining main street, she saw beauty and renewal.

She leaned forward in the passenger's seat trying to capture it all as it passed across the window like a winter carnival. The brilliance of mid-winter was never more glorious.

They reached her apartment. She hadn't paid much attention to the old building before. She looked at the black shutters on the windows of the brick building. It comforted her to think they would shelter her from a storm. Even the worn mailbox was charming, a small replica of an old Vermont barn, now faded from its former bright red exterior with the faded white *3809 Murphy*. Bud had secured a new larger apartment on the second floor and she scaled the stairs rapidly.

Brigid made a salad—chickpeas, beans, lentils, cucumbers—part of the new restricted diet Shannon would have to eat for the rest of her life. It was delicious after weeks of bland hospital food and she savored every bite. They sat close together at the small kitchen table.

"Brig' I don't think I can ever tell you how grateful I am for your sacrifice. Leaving Joe and moving in with me to make me whole again. I don't know if I can ever find a way to…."

"Hey, Shan.' Don't fret about any of that. I want you around for a long time. I am thrilled to see you so healthy."

Shannon abruptly stood, bent over Brigid, and wrapped her arms around her. Brigid had been used to just the occasional brief hand across the shoulder. It was the first time her sister had ever hugged her.

"What's the matter?"

"I just felt like a hug. I know, unlike me. But I am forever grateful to you."

"I can see that. I do love you, you know. I have a big surprise…for us!"

"Surprise? I'm already full of surprises just being back here in East Cabot is exciting."

"I am taking us on a winter vacation. There's a beautiful quaint Inn about two hours from here in upstate New York that I have always wanted to visit. And now's the perfect time. You're healthy enough to travel and I have the extra money I saved from selling my condo. It's a tidy sum and I can't think of a better way to spend some of it. It's my Valentine's to you."

"Sounds wonderful. What's the place?"

"The Round Top Barn Inn. Out in the country near those beautiful Siamese Ponds Wilderness you used to talk about. Normally booked a year in advance. They had a special on a suite in February when few people visit. I thought we could take some hikes. They have cleared trails for hikers. Great food. Called ahead to make sure they have stuff you can eat. And no TV, no internet. Just solace."

"Brig' that's so perfect. When will we leave?"

"Day after tomorrow. Tomorrow's Valentine's day. Until then, you need to rest and get used to things here. I imagine you're exhausted."

"You know, Brig' I'm not tired at all. I have energy. But I'll rest and make sure I follow orders."

Shannon called Bud Travis at the *Caledonian* to let him know they were back in the new apartment and that she was well and eager to come back, she thought by early spring. She wanted to start writing again and would take a notebook with her on the vacation. Her head was swirling with new ideas, but they were jumbled together, almost nonsense.

They stayed up late, talking about the past weeks, what lay ahead, the family they shared.

"Mom would have been so proud of you, Shan'."

"Yeah, I miss Mom. Especially now I know what she had gone through. Back then, they didn't have heart transplants. And I loved our home in Burrs Oaks. I wonder what ever happened to that old place? It was run down by the time we left, but what memories! I can just picture it now."

"Yeah, I remember how our street was lined with those big lush maples, so pretty in October. Our big backyard overlooking the neighbor homes. Especially Bobby Purcell. Remember him? I had the biggest crush on that boy," Brigid said.

"Bobby, oh yes! I wonder what ever happened to his dog."

"Dog? I don't remember a dog. When was that?"

"He had this pretty Cocker Spaniel, black and white. I can picture him right now. Sweet dog."

"You sure? I can't recall his dog."

"Yes. I remember how Bobby and his mother used to fuss over him. His name was 'Skipper.' When we were kids, the dog was old, think about fourteen or so. Old. I remember the day they found him in the back yard. The poor old dog had walked out there late one night and just cured up next to his dog house and died."

Her eyes filled with tears.

"We lived in that house together for so long, but I don't remember that dog, Shan'."

"Oh yes! That dog meant everything to Bobby. I remember him kneeling over that lifeless little dog, cradling his head as he rocked back and forth, sobbing for hours."

Brigid stared at her. Her brow furled.

"I can't believe you remember something like *that*."

"Well, it's in my memory. Not sure what jogged that."

The rest of the evening was spent in silence as the sisters readied for bed.

A snowstorm blanketed East Cabot that night. As the snow fell through the gray skies, Shannon lay in bed sleepily watching the flakes silently drift against her window. A blue light from the streetlamp flickered across the ceiling of her bedroom as she lay in a reverie.

Sometime in the depths of the night, she came up out of a darkness that was not sleep but something else, something more vast and comforting, the darkness of willful unconsciousness like the first awakening of a baby from the womb. She sensed a breath against her, a slow and warm pulsing at her cheek. The smell of it filled her, its sweet warm stink. The comfort of it pulled her further into the reverie. Something soft pressed against her, clinging to her, its weight familiar. She breathed deeply against it, holding it, protecting it as it shifted through the night.

Intense sunlight flooded the room. She opened her eyes. The storm had passed and the sky was brilliant, a blue that hurt the most sensitive eyes.

She shifted her head about in the bed, her arms feeling along the covers. Nothing was there, not even a hint of something.

The sleep had been deep and long. She bounded out of bed. Her sister called from the living room.

"Hey sleepy, you've been out!"

Brigid opened her bedroom door. Shannon was at the window, sun washing across her face.

"I had the strangest…I mean, I must have had a dream or something."

"What was it, Shan?"

"I don't know. It was a feeling. Immensely comforting. I don't even think it was a dream."

Shannon stared out into the white landscape that rose above the tops of homes like a majestic tableau against a cloudless sky. Sparrows cartwheeled like spinning bullets against the blue canvas. From the far field, a killdeer bird chattered his bright winter song *kee-dee, kee-dee.* Soft plumes of smoke rose from chimneys and the many red Christmas ribbons still hung on the doors.

She had never witnessed East Cabot in such an exquisite way. It was as if the whole town had blossomed in her chest. And with it, the reverie from the night.

Brigid stood in the doorway, her cup filled with Mister Coffee. Her heart raced.

"Are you okay? You look so far away."

Shannon didn't answer. The fantasy lingered. It was foreign yet familiar, frightening but reassuring. She felt detached but somehow a part of everything.

"Oh Brig.' I wish I could tell you how comforted I feel right now. I don't know why, but it's so wonderful. Like nothing I've ever felt. And I look so forward to going up to Round Top Barn."

Her sister let out a long held breath.

"Whew! For a minute, I was afraid I was losing you there. Want some coffee? Oh wait, you're not supposed to drink that stuff. OJ?"

"Let's take a walk into town today. Let's get out into this beautiful snow," she said still looking out the window.

Overnight, a foot of new powder had blanketed East Cabot. The sisters pushed through the thick white drifts with their bright new boots. Shannon was amazed. She hadn't walked in deep snow since she was young. She remembered the town in winters past. The miserable cold, the dirty snow piles in front of dilapidated, empty storefronts, the peeling spire of the East Cabot church, closed-for-winter signs. And the darkness, the constant gloomy grey everywhere. She remembered how the sunlight would slowly disappear from the streets as the winter sun moved lower and lower along the distant hills and how she'd wait for days, weeks, even a month, to get back just a small hope of light, but then melting snows and rain in the early spring would soak everything with dirty mud and slush, and the unpaved streets would become undrivable and she'd remain inside, again waiting for the 'real' spring to find relief. All of it weighted down by a constant heaviness from a sick heart.

That had all changed now.

She took in a deep breath and smiled. Everything was new and bright. Even the smells were different. She was a child again, discovering everything anew. She loved how East Cabot looked.

They crunched smoothly through the thick snowdrifts as they turned back to the apartment.

An ordinary morning had passed. For Brigid at least. But for Shannon, everything was remarkable. And what she felt most was comfort but she didn't understand why. She was still the same witty woman who always seem to view the world in words and phrases. And this morning was a long phrase, a series of extraordinary sentences. Yes, she felt alive and healthy, but that wasn't quite it.

Something stirred in her, something she felt she must do.

Something she was being told to do.

8

Shannon twisted in her seat as the Round Top Barn Inn came into view. The large white structure was topped off with an impressive, perfectly round red dome. It had been built in 1804 by Clem Joslyn, a religious farmer who wanted the building to be free of devils that could hide in corners. The effect was terrific.

Brigid's car had barely rolled to a stop before Shannon flew out the door, landing in a snowdrift, kicking and laughing as she stared upside down at the Inn.

"It's so perfect!"

Their small cottage sat on a hill behind the inn with a panoramic view of the distant mountains and into valley below. The living room had wrap-around windows from an old barn with grey weathered wood and century-old black latches. It was a clear day and you could see over eighty miles in the distance across the Merrimack Valley into the state of Vermont. The far hills were powder-sugared, layer upon layer of pure white, a scene from an old-fashioned Christmas card.

Shannon stared out at the view and said:

"Our snow was not only shaken from whitewash buckets down the sky, it came shawling out of the ground and swam and drifted out of the arms and hands and bodies of the trees. Snow overnight on the roofs of the houses like a pure and grandfather moss, minutely white ivied the walls and settled on the postman opening the gate like a numb, dumb thunderstorm of white torn Christmas cards."

"Wow, that's beautiful, Shan'!"

"Yes, thanks to Dylan Thomas. Described perfectly in his *Child's Christmas in Wales.*"

They relaxed in plush chairs facing the windows, the sun in their faces. They were miles from any towns or neighbors. The silence was beautiful.

"I can't wait to hike," Shannon finally said.

"Well, it's a bit late and cold out there now. Tomorrow's supposed to be clear. We can go in the morning. We have three days here. I just wanted you to relax and enjoy the peace."

Brigid took a nap, but Shannon was restless and decided to walk along the hill where their cottage sat. At edge of the hill, she looked into the valley. Faint mist was rolling back from the tall Norway pines that lined spots along its length. Within the dense evergreens, she could just make out some half-hidden buildings far in the distance below.

In the silence, she heard a dog bark, a ghost-like far-off sound, a bright bark, just one. She cocked her head and closed her eyes but it had stopped. The vision from two nights earlier swept across her. She felt the warmth, the familiar weight against her.

From the valley below, a cold wind swept up and over her. She turned back.

It was late afternoon and Chauncey was outside in the CAS field with Dru working on her retrieving skills. She was well ahead of Dru in the large field. She had dropped the orange retrieving dummy and was frozen in a point, as if she had suddenly spotted a bird or squirrel in the brush. Her front paw lifted in a gentle bend and her back hocks gathered. But her head was pointed upward, to the hills beyond. Her nose quivered wildly. Chauncey's rear legs began to quiver and she stepped back and let out a bright bark. Her tail swung wildly. Dru approached her and knelt. The dog shivered and began pacing about, whining softly. Dru looked around but couldn't see anything. The fields and paths were empty.

Early that first morning, the sisters took the Red Path trail west towards the Siamese Ponds Wilderness. It was twenty degrees but being late February, the winter solstice had loosened its grip and the sun hung higher in the sky. Shannon walked ahead, her red knit cap bobbing as she hurried along the narrow trail lined with the boughs of firs weighted down with their thick white pillows. The trail climbed to a point overlooking the twin Siamese Ponds, the larger shaped like a huge bird in flight swooping gently to its smaller twin. They reached the pinnacle and looked down at the blue-green waters shimmering in the cold air. Shannon leaned forward as if she heard something in the distance. It had gone, that feeling of warmth and softness that she had felt yesterday.

Brigid watched her sister as she stood at the edge of the steep cliff. How beautiful she looked! Her bright eyes reflected the color of the sky, almost a turquoise or even like the Delft blue of her Dutch statuettes. Shannon's brow was furled and her small bow lips were slightly open as if she were speaking to someone. But she was speaking to nobody, maybe to the wind, asking for something. It was a look she had never seen before. She almost didn't recognize her sister yet she looked like someone she wanted to know, wanted to love.

Brigid stepped towards her. Shannon stood quietly in the breeze, her head tilted, her eyes closed.

"Are you enjoying the moment?"

There was no response for a minute. She turned and smiled.

"Yes. It's indescribable. I should write down my thoughts."

She reached into her parka and pulled out a pencil and notebook and sat on the large granite cliff, immersed in thought. Her sister left her alone and walked along the far ridge.

After an hour, the cold got to Brigid and she returned.

"We need to get back. Did you get much written?"

"It's nonsense. I have to make it out. It'll be better when we're warm and I can think more clearly. Jumbled up right now."

On the first page of her notebook was written several lines, all of which were crossed out except one:

A promise to you who is alone.

Just outside the Inn, they reached the crest of another hill. Shannon stopped. On the opposite far ridge, she noticed something moving in the distance, something running along the line of dark trees, an animal, its bright feathers floating in the wind. It stopped and turned towards her, the morning sun radiating gold against it.

She leaned forward but in seconds, it was gone.

"My God, did you see that?" Shannon said.

"What?"

"Right there!"

She pointed out to the far ridge.

Brigid craned her neck forward. The landscape was still.

"I don't see anything. What was it?"

"I don't know exactly. It was there, just right there, just for a second. But it's gone now. Oh, where did it go?"

"I didn't see anything. Are you sure you're feeling okay?"

"We need to go over there."

"Are you kidding me? You can't get over there!"

Brigid grabbed her sister's mitten and pulled her away.

"We have to go back. The cold is getting to me. Please!"

In the Inn, they sat by the fire. Brigid hesitated to say anything after her sister's absurd request. Shannon stared into the flames. Reflections of gold rippled across her serious face.

"Something has changed in me, Brigid. I can't say what. I just feel different. I don't understand it, but it's there. I have to find a way to write this down."

Brigid stared at her. She wasn't sure how to respond. Shannon always knew how to find her way through things. She had walked through near-death. Surely, she can make it through whatever was happening to her now. But this frightened her.

"I think I need a drink!" Brigid said and laughed.

"Great idea. I can have my one for the month."

Red wine was served and they drank hardily and laughed.

That night, Chauncey lay awake next to Callie in their pen. From her pen, she could just see out the window towards the valley and hills beyond. Her quivering nose pulled in many scents. The musty smell of Callie, bedbugs somewhere, Dr. Farnum's tumor, fear from someone at CAS, perhaps Dru, juniper and pine, the remnants of beef dinner, a young moose wandering close by.

As the night passed and while she moved in and out of sleep, a new scent aroused her. It was distinct. Familiar. She rose, walked to the pen's edge, and pulled in the air. She began barking.

The facility lights illuminated. Dru was in her pajamas, running down the hallway.

"What's the matter, girl?"

She opened the pen door and crouched down. Chauncey crawled onto her and tucked head into her legs. She whined softly.

"What is it, girl? Are you sick?"

She grabbed the first aid kit from the wall and took Chauncey's temperature. Normal. She looked at her gums, felt her flanks. She looked okay but her dog paced the hallway, looking for an exit.

Dru led her out but she just stood in the back fenced yard, staring out to the dark hills beyond. She took Chauncey back to her room, but she spent the night with little sleep.

A good night's rest helped put things back into perspective and the next morning, Shannon felt less confused, more directed, anxious to get back home and begin writing. They had that morning and early afternoon to enjoy hiking before the two-hour drive home.

Today, Shannon wanted to hike the ridge along the Inn to take in the valley view out towards Baker's Mills. Another clear day, rare for February, known for its fierce weather. It would snow late that night, but they'd be home by then.

Their marked trail wound along the old Person's Road, which had been closed for some years. They had been out for two hours and had gone off to a side trail that led them further down the ridge closer towards the valley where they could just make out some of Baker's Mills and to its right, the same buildings Shannon had seen the first day. As they descended the trail, a stiff wind picked up from the ridge behind them, sweeping over them and down into the valley.

Brigid looked at her watch: 2:05 p.m.

"We need to leave by three before the storm hits this evening."

"Sure, okay. Let's go back."

Shannon turned back to follow Brigid but something caught her attention. Off to her left. A far-off sound. She stopped and looked down into the valley. *Maybe just the trees rubbing together*, she thought, and continued to trudge back up the hill. Again, the silence was pierced. It had come from the large building below in the valley. It sounded like a bark. She looked down but the thick stand of firs obscured the buildings. Then, another bark reached her, this one sharp and loud and she could just make out something running through the firs, and then disappear.

She waited, listened.

"Hey, Shan'—let's get going. I don't want to drive back in the dark."

Shannon's heart raced. It was beating faster than it should have for just this hike. Her chest felt heavy. In her mind's eye, she could see the image of the day before, the animal on the ridge. Something stirred within her, a feeling like she needed to do something. Something left undone.

They packed the car and drove off.

Dru and the dogs were on a hike along the paths in back of CAS. It was just before 2 p.m. and Chauncey was off leash wearing her tracking collar. She was ahead of them, stopping every few feet, sniffing the air. She barked. Again, a bright bark. She was barely visible between a stand of firs. She barked a third time, loud and sharp, and raced forward.

"Chauncey…Chauncey!" Dru yelled.

Callie looked up. She knew something was wrong. Dru opened her tracking tablet. Chauncey's signal was accurate for up to two miles. The blinking dot placed her ahead several hundred feet, but in the wilderness, distances were deceptive. The dot was moving away rapidly, up towards the mountain. She buzzed the collar to call her dog back but there was no response.

"Chauncey!"

The dot was now a mile away. Dru couldn't keep up and collapsed in the snow. Callie crawled on her lap.

She watched the blinking dot flicker and then disappear.

9

By the time Chauncey had reached the summit, the smell that had drawn her had faded. She raced back and forth along the path, desperately trying to locate the scent but was now uncertain.

It was dusk and the temperature had dropped to twelve degrees. She looked down the mountain at the brightly lit CAS buildings. It was many miles away and she was exhausted.

She ran in further and she reached several large buildings, one with a round dome silhouetted against the dark sky. The building had one small light from a window. A night attendant was closing the Inn. With no more reservations until spring, it had closed down.

She sampled the air. The smell was stronger here. Just off to her right, up another small hill.

She climbed through the snowdrifts to a small cottage and climbed up the stairs, her nose to the floor. Here, the smell was distinct. She whined, pacing along the cottage porch.

Exhaustion overcame her and she circled into a bed of snow.

She looked out at the unfamiliar darkness and closed her eyes, but here, in this unknown place, there was nobody to help her and she had little peace.

That night, she dreamed of Dirck. It had been over four months since he had left her, but tonight, his memory was close. She pictured him running across the field towards her, shifting his hands, left and right, signaling to her this way and that, and then clapping in the air to signal her back. She remembered that she loved to break into a run just because she knew that he loved to watch her ears flapping in the wind.

She heard barking. Someone called for her. Was it Dirck? She let out a yelp and opened her eyes. It was not a dream. The storm had broken and in the faint morning light, she saw a dog running towards her, barking wildly. It was Callie. Behind her, three people ran up the path.

Dru spotted her. Dave and a trainer were behind them. The tracking tablet had found her.

"Chauncey!"

She leapt off the cottage porch into Dru's open arms, crying, licking her cheeks, begging for forgiveness. Why had she gone? Why was she here? Callie ran in circles around them all, barking her happiness to everyone.

She fastened Chauncey's harness and lead.

"Why did you run off like that, girl? Why were you up here?" said Dru.

"She seems to have been drawn to something up here. Let me look around," said Dave.

They traversed the trail and around the buildings, letting the dog lead them. Suddenly, Chauncey jerked Dave off to her left towards the Inn.

"Where are we going, girl? What's over here?"

Chauncey pulled him to the front of the Inn and stopped. She sat in the snow and stared into the distance. Dru looked down. In front of her dog were faint tire marks leading down the hill.

"There was a car here recently. Someone who dove off last night before the storm from the looks of the tracks. What drew her here?" said Dru.

"Damned if I know. She's obviously sensing something but the Inn's closed and there's no way to find out who had been here."

Chauncey sampled the air, trying, in vain, to find some trace of the familiar smell.

"We need to get her back, Dave—she's exhausted and must be confused. That was a long and steep climb. I can't believe she made it by herself."

They hiked down into the valley to CAS.

Again, and again, Chauncey stopped and turned back towards the crest of the hill and pulled in the air.

But her resolve was gone.

10

Mud season had descended on East Cabot as it had on all of Vermont with its rich odors from muddy roads and dank interiors and numerous calls for tow trucks to again pull out tourists from their ill-advised back-road adventures.

It was late April and despite the melted mush and mud, Vermont was beautiful as ever, at least to Shannon as she looked out from her upstairs window.

She laughed under her breath at Mr. Jilly as he cursed his truck stuck again in a deep rut in his driveway.

"Stuck again? Sorry. I can get ahold of a tow for you," she yelled at the man from across the street.

"Na, Shannon. Got some boards in the back. That'll do 'er. Damned snow melted off too fast last night. But thanks."

She watched the stout man shove flat boards under his truck.

Jilly's Village Store was the only reseller left in East Cabot. The place occupied the first floor of Gerald and Mildred Jilly's house. The sign on their porch read

If we don't have it,
you don't need it!

And it was true. Jilly's store looked small from the front but it ran the entire length of the deep property. Inside, rows of shelves and tables were layered with muck boots and tools, bedroom and barn doors of all sizes, odd kitchen utensils, dyeing fabrics, cleaners and spot removers, bird houses large and small, bathroom plungers and zippo lighters, and everything Vermont—Cabot maple syrup, Angry Goat Jams, Red Kite Candies, Ben and Jerry's, Yankee Candles, East Cabot fudge, Grafton Cheddar. One was never empty-handed at Jilly's. Gerald Jilly had run the place for more than twenty years and everyone in the region knew the hardworking man and Mildred, his stout wife of thirty years.

There were two customers in the store that morning. Mikey, the local kid that came in each morning for coffee and Gerry Michaels from the East Cabot Town office delivering Jilly's yearly license renewal.

"Poor man," Mildred said to Gerry as she watched her husband struggle to shove boards under his tires in the deep mud.

She noticed Shannon looking on from her apartment window across the street.

"Oh, there's Shannon up there. That girl's so kind. Always lookin' out for us. Damned shame about that big problem she had with her heart. Heard it was okay now. Looks a lot better, just like the Shannon we used to know," said Mildred.

"Yes, glad to see she's on a good road now," said Gerry who had moved to the other front window to watch. "Poor woman has been through a ton in life."

Mildred turned to her.

"How-so?"

"Knew two of her cousins from Burrs Oaks who worked at the old Woolen Mill there. They grew up around that Murphy family. Poor girl went through some rough things," said Gerry.

"What happened?"

"Quite a time ago when Shannon was a young girl, her father died a bad death, drinkin' and all. Mean man. That girl wanted so bad to get close to him but he just pushed her away—some say even abused the poor girl—and one day, story goes, he just up and died right in front of her sittin' in his rocker, not even recognizing his own daughter. That shut her down good. For years, she didn't speak to anyone 'cept her mother. The girl wouldn't even let anyone touch her."

"Oh, I never knew."

"Yeah, then finally one day, her cousins and some of the folk around town felt so bad they got together and bought her a dog. A pretty little white lab pup, I remember. Sweet thing. She took care of that little dog. I mean she fed him, even made him a bed in their barn, but you know somethin'? She never once really touched that pup—never even held him or pet him."

Gerry shook her head as she stared at Shannon form across the street.

"She just couldn't touch anything she cared about. They said the further she stayed away from anyone, the more protected she felt. That never really left her."

Mildred looked at her and nodded.

"Well, that explains things. I knew she was with this local carpenter fella early on but heard he just took off. Rumor was he had found another girl. Don't think I remember her ever huggin' anyone. She always seemed kind of lost that way. Gerald thought so too."

"Yeah, she finally moved away from Burrs Oaks when her mother passed. Came here to start a new life with that nice sister of her's. Brigid. Now, *that* girl's a hugger. Together, they look more like distant cousins. Never showin' any affection and all. Sad really. I heard the sister plans to go back off to her old place now that Shannon's better."

The two women continued staring out the window. Gerald Jilly had his truck loose now. Shannon waved and smiled at the women. They raised their hands to acknowledge her.

The next day, Shannon walked to the *Caledonian Record.* It had been nearly six months since she had been there. Bud Travis was in his back office and saw some woman talking to one of the paper's editors.

He walked out towards her. Shannon turned to him.

"Hi! Great to see you again, Bud!"

The voice jolted him into recognition.

"Shannon? By God, it *is* you. You look…great!"

The woman before him bore no resemblance to the bloated heavyset woman he had last seen in her apartment last fall. She displayed a trim figure and was energetic.

"Strange, I almost expected to see this place shut down without any decent writing talent!"

She flashed Bud a wry smile.

"Oh, you got that right. I've had to do much of it for the past few months. A tough assignment to follow in your wake."

Bud moved forward to hug her but stopped short, remembering the last time when Shannon had stepped away from him. He put his hand on her shoulder in a pathetic stage of affection. She grabbed it and pulled him in for a hug.

"Well, no more assignments for you, Bud. I want to get started right away," she said as she squeezed him.

"Perfect. I have an idea that our readers have been asking about. Come back and we'll go over it."

Fifteen years earlier, when she was first hired as the editor at the *Caledonian*, she was asked to finish the op-ed by then-editor Johnny Murray, about East Cabot's rise and demise. Bud explained he now wanted to expand that into a monthly series. The fading history of Vermont. He wanted to feature stories about the families, the estates, the forgotten places. It was to be a personal love story of Vermont, a story that's never before been told. The way only Shannon could write it.

"Still sharp, I take it?" Bud asked as he stared across his desk at her.

"Sharper. Mind's cleared of worry."

"Wonderful. I'd like you to start around this area. Towns of East Cabot, Pownal, North Pownal, Groton. And up to Glenriver and surrounding area. Fascinating history there. And beautiful, mostly rural."

"I am getting a new car next week so I can start on some background from the folks around these areas. The libraries and town halls. Not sure of the timing, but I can probably get you episodes at least once each month. Maybe more."

"We got you a cellphone so we can keep in touch. It's set up already."

It was modern phone with maps, internet connection, the works. He handed it to her.

"I really appreciate that, Bud. It'll help with the research. Never sure when places are open or people available."

She walked back home the four long blocks along Danville Hill Road. It would soon be May and recent warm weather had delivered lilacs, tulips, and daffodils displaying their cheerful colors along the otherwise drab grey fences and stone walls.

She approached Ernie Jacob's house and spotted his teenaged daughter, Agnes, on the porch swing. There was a dog lying next to her.

"Hi Agnes. How's Dad?"

"Shannon? Is that you? You look different! Dad's in the back. Want me to get him?"

"Nope. Just passing by."

The older black Labrador rose unsteadily to his feet and waged his tail as she approached.

"Don't remember you having a dog. How long have you had him?"

The girl stared at her.

"Uh, like twelve years. Since he was a puppy. You've seen him before, many times."

"Don't remember. What's his name?"

"Buddy. He's friendly, a big softie."

She walked up the short stoop and knelt. Buddy ambled slowly to her and lightly licked her outreached hand. A calm swept through her. She reached for the dog's head but stopped to ask permission.

"It's ok. He always loves a good pet."

The dog stared at Shannon. His eyes were cloudy and watering and his muzzle grey, but she could tell his spirit was strong and sweet. His butt wiggled as she held him. She stroked the dog's slobbery muzzle and closed her eyes. That feeling again swept over her. Comfort, something warm and soft against her.

She opened her eyes. Buddy looked at up at her, his eyes steady and reassuring.

"Wow, Buddy really likes you. He's not like that with people."

"Tell your dad I stopped by," Shannon said as she stoked Buddy's face.

As she walked back to the sidewalk, Buddy let out a chesty *ruff*. She turned and held her hand up.

"You be a good boy, Buddy. I'll be back."

The next morning, Shannon sat on the tiny cement deck of her apartment scribbling ideas into a notebook. She was ready to travel through the state. As expected that day, a driver showed up with a new dark-green Subaru Forester. The paperwork had been completed and signed and the dealer picked up the young salesman and drove off, leaving the new car parked in front of her apartment. She was ready to go.

She couldn't even remember the last time she drove a car.

She had already written one piece on East Cabot and by eight that morning, she drove to Pownal and the two miles to North Pownal, both with just the one Town Office.

"Hello, I'm Shannon Murphy, chief editor at the *Caledonian Record* and I'd like to look at your historical files."

The young clerk checked her picture ID and led her to a large walk-in vault. There were dozens of thick books, each with dates: 1760-1780, 1781-1790 through the last record of 2007.

"Don't yet have the transcriptions after that later date."

"I'm looking for the older ones, anyway."

She sat at the metal table going through each book. They contained detailed accounts of the town, all written in fancy cursive style using a quill and ink.

After an hour, she wrote:

On January 8, 1760 John C. Pownall III chartered the town together with his brother, Thomas H. Pownall. A fight in the legislature ensued and the town councilmen voted to drop the final 'l' to name the town 'Pownal.' Two Presidents taught in Pownal at the beginning of their careers—Chester A. Arthur educated Pownal youth as did James A. Garfield. But when Garfield was assassinated in 1881, Arthur succeeded him. You can still see the marker to this fact near the North Pownal Congregational church. The town, and its cousin 'North Pownal' was home to scandal, an unsolved murder, a popular racetrack, and a terrific hurricane in the 1930s that ripped out all the tall walnut trees lining the town green, nearly wiping the town off the early rich Vermont map. Billy Ferral, now nearly ninety years of age, says that as a boy, he watched the trees as they flew from the ground, like in the Wizard of Oz, the winds lifting his young life away.

It wasn't her best writing but after filling ten pages in her notebook, stories of the town's beginning, its demise and rebirth, and scandals began to emerge like a novel, a mystery really. She returned home and put together a first part of the series "A Terrible Beauty—Vermont's Forgotten People."

That next day she drove to Groton in Caledonia County. Groton was much the same as Pownal with its Town Offices and historic records and hidden history.

Late that day, she travelled the forty miles from Groton up to Glenriver, a small rural town. Although the town was listed in the annals of history, it wasn't on any tourist destination and was known only to the few long-standing neighbors and the local historical society.

As she turned onto Route 44, she spotted the serene town green. Along it and up Route 44 stood stately historic homes, most antebellum, all built in the early 1800's.

Something about the place seemed familiar, intimate.

She parked and walked up the green. Few people were out this early May day but off the green, she spotted a woman bent over a garden in the back of a large house. She walked up the driveway with its hand-painted sign *Bristoll's.*

"Hello. Hope I'm not intruding. I'd like your help."

A small woman dressed in dirty overalls was crouched over some white daffodils. She looked up. The woman was probably close to ninety but looked ageless. Her house was a stately Federal Style structure, simple frame and clapboard, U-shaped, two stories high and two rooms deep with four chimneys on an aging slate roof. It was grand yet understated.

Something about the home and Sarah seemed recognizable. The woman climbed to her feet.

"Ah-yep. I'm Sarah Bristoll. Wha' can I do ya' for?"

"My name's Shannon Murphy from East Cabot. Work for the *Caledonian Record.* I'm writing stories of Vermont's history."

"Oh, yep, East Cabot, have some cousins down theyah. Nice place down Cabot way. Know tha' paper, too. Good one."

She recognized the woman's distinct Vermont accent. She was probably a second or third generation Vermonter.

"Yes, it's nice town. I'm trying to get some history of Glenriver but know you don't have a town office here. Are there any historic records you know of?"

"A-yep. The charter went to Brimstone Corners up north a-hereah. But John Poindexter keeps a bunch of records and pictures down in back of the library on the town green. You could start theyah—tell him Sarah Bristoll sent you on. Lots-a history to be sure."

"Wonderful, I very much appreciate that and I hope your daffodils open soon."

"Always do. White variety. Been growin' hereah way before I was born in this very house."

Shannon tried to imagine Sarah Bristoll as a young girl back at the turn of the century in this old home. She imagined everything here looked much the same back then as it did now. The thought comforted her.

She thanked the woman but as she turned, the house next door caught her eye. It looked large and inviting, familiar.

She turned and walked back the short distance to the library on the green.

To one side of the larger library in a separate entrance, an entrance was marked *Glenriver Historical Society.* Inside, at a small desk sat an older man reading a book. His thick white hair was smartly combed back and he wore a short-sleeved white shirt with a neatly tied red bowtie. His thin wire-framed glasses sat on his crook-like nose. She thought he looked old but people in this part of the world were deceptively young in spirit and presence.

He looked up and smiled.

"Ah-yeah, hello young lady," he said.

"Good morning. Are you Mr. Poindexter? My name is Shannon Murphy from East Cabot. I'm here to do some research on Glenriver and surrounding area. Your neighbor, Sarah Bristoll, told me to see you. I wonder if you might show me some historical records you have of the towns here."

"Yep, Miss Bristoll. I'm Poindexter. I have many records hereah."

He slowly stood up and walked to the back of the narrow room where he opened a wooden cabinet to reveal rows of drawers, each neatly hand-labeled with town names, dates, people.

"Start hereah in this drawer. Has some early files of Glenriver and we can go from theyah through some other records."

She pulled out a drawer and sat at the long wooden table carefully reading each record. Deeds, letters, copies of town charter were neatly arranged with clips.

The first record was a deed from Theodore Benson, a local magistrate who had founded Glenriver on August 12, 1761 by way of a royal charter issued to Governor Benning Wordsworth of New Hampshire. Benson had originally named it Thetford, for an Augustus Fitzroy of Grafston, fourth Viscount Thetford, but as the town grew, and its people protested England's involvement, they renamed it *Glenriver* after the oldest inhabitant, Glen Tenny, who lived at the edge of the town's only river. She was barely able to read the browned script writing. It had been written by a perfectly preserved white feathered quill, also in the collection, the point still blacked from its last record.

It was well after 1 p.m. when she reached the end of the stack. She started to put the drawer back but noticed one larger drawer at the bottom of the cabinet. Inside were white envelopes, each hand-lettered with dates and places. She pulled out one stack. They contained dark copper plates with photographic images, each separated with tissues. The images had been made over one hundred years earlier by a local photographer who had first learned a new technique called the *daguerreotype*. They all had a mirror-like, silvery-gold surface and were high resolution.

"Oh, miss, you'll have to be put on gloves for them photographs," said Poindexter.

"Gloves?"

"Yep. Daguerreotypes are delicate, even the lightest pressure with oils from your hand will ruin those plates."

She carefully donned the white gloves Poindexter handed her and carefully began to remove the photographs from their edges, placing them in rows along the table. Handling them with white gloves seemed to give them a magical quality. They almost seemed to glow with a coppery-gold hue.

There were images of people in groups standing on the green, in front of the Congregational church, along their homes, others showing the impressive newly built homes. The buildings were in sharp focus but many of the people were blurred because the exposures were 30 seconds or longer. Penned on the back of each was a date. Shannon examined them closely.

Poindexter stood at the table watching her. He was a guardian of the town and had spent his life protecting Glenriver's history. He pointed to one photo and smiled.

"Tha' is the old Church, still out hereah off the green. Was the focal point of the district and sat on the green back then. These townspeople hereah moved it across the road from the north end of the common in 1820. By hand. On logs. Was the town church and meetinghouse. Town gatherings has happened every March first for the past hundred or so years now."

Shannon pulled out photographs of the homes along the green and up Route 44. One had several views of the front and side. She leaned forward.

"What's this beautiful home?"

"That's the old Judge Benson homestead. Grand home, true antebellum."

Theodore Benson, a local magistrate who had founded Glenriver, built the homestead two hundred years earlier and at the homestead's front, she could just make out the weathered sign *JUDGE BENSON'S HOUSE 1807.* There were more photographs of the homestead. She placed them along the table in some order, trying to make some sense of them. The images showed a large house that stood back from the road almost hidden amongst the handsome firs and spruce. Glimpses could be caught of the sprawling yard and meadows beyond. An old driveway lined with brilliant white birches meandered through wide-spreading lawns. The images glowed with the brilliance of the first images of the homestead.

She leaned forward. Something about the place looked familiar and felt oddly reassuring.

"Who lived here at the Judge's house over the years?"

"Oh, tha' place has a history to be surah'. Let's see, a-course the judge himself lived theyah as a young man when he founded the town. Lived at tha' house until about sixty-odd years afta' the civil war, I believe. Then moved out to the old George Sayre's place. Then came Latham and Kendhall for a spell. All the while, there was no road in front hereah, just fields for cows to graze. They had to put up tha' fence to keep them from eatin' the planted flowers and such."

She picked up one photograph showing the home from the front road.

"Yeah, then in the 1900s, others took it over, don't rememba' their names. Sometime in the 1930's or 1940's, Douglas Hansen bought the place. Famous Army Colonel. Handsome fella.' Then he willed the place to his son, Dirck, when he passed on."

"Where does that house sit in relationship to the green?"

"Just up the old Route 44, just 'bout four houses up from where we sit."

That was the house she had seen earlier next door to Sarah Bristoll.

"Who lives there now?"

"Don't rightly know. Believe the fella that lived there, Douglas's son, Dirck, passed on and not surah' who lives there now, if anyone. Haven't seen much activity 'round tha' place in months. Walk past it every day for my exercise. Looks empty now."

She pointed to one of the photographs.

"What's this of?"

"That's a shot of the back area lookin' away from the house. The fields and Glenriver Town Forest. Not surah' why that's interesting."

It wasn't remarkable yet the photograph drew her in.

"Did Mr. Hansen, I mean the son who lived there, did he live there alone?"

"Yes ma'am, he was a bachelor. Lived theyah alone pretty much. He and his dog."

"His dog?" Shannon looked up at him.

"Yep. Golden Retriever type pup. Protected him—he had tha' war trauma from his duty ova' there in Iraq. Dog was a service-type pooch. Did a good job keepin' him alive. Big story 'bout him and tha' dog was in the Glenriver paper some years ago. Dog had been lost for a good while, maybe a couple years, then returned home. Caught some fella robbin' him. Quite a tale."

"You say Dirck Hansen passed on? Do you know what happened to him…to his dog?"

"Don't rightly know, ma'am. Paper said he passed last fall, I believe. Don' know much about tha' dog."

"Are there more recent photographs of the home?"

"Oh, we have many years' worth. Not sura' how recent. Let me see...."

Poindexter opened a cabinet on the opposite wall with rows of drawers. He pulled out a large lower drawer.

"Yep, these are the last shots we have. Maybe 'bout twelve or so years old."

He took out two large envelopes labeled "Glenriver Homes, 2000-2006."

The photographs were larger, all in color. He spread them out on the table with the older photographs.

"Do you have any of this Judge Benson's homestead?"

"Yep. There's some in here."

There were thirty photographs, all taken various years of different places. He spread them out on the table.

Five of the photographs were of the Benson homestead. One was the rear of the house showing a small stone patio. A man was seated in one of the chairs, his legs crossed, smiling at the camera. A dog sat by his side, looking up at him. She brought it up and examined it closely.

"Oh, this one—is this the man and his dog—the veteran Hansen and his service dog?"

Poindexter moved his glasses on his forehead and leaned forward.

"Yep. That's Dirck Hansen fella and his dog. Think tha' was when he first brought tha' dog home. Sara Ferguson took that, I believe. She used to visit him sometimes. She's gone too now, you know."

"Do you know what that dog's name was?"

It seemed like an odd question. But Poindexter knew she was a reporter and without answering her, he went to another cabinet and pulled out some newspaper clippings. He lowered his glasses and read one clipping.

"Hereah. Story says…name's *Chauncey*.

She looked over his shoulder. The newspaper clipping labeled *Glenriver Courier Journal* was a two-page account of the man and his dog. He handed it to Shannon.

"Like I said. Tha' dog was a godsend to tha' Hansen fella. They think that dog was stolen but it found its way back home hereah."

The story's titled *Brave Dog Saves Veteran*. She read it intently and then leaned back into the chair, out of breath. Her heart began to race.

"You okay, young lady?"

She brought a hand to her mouth. Her eyes teared up. She looked back down at the clipping.

The story ended:

Dirck Hansen nearly died that night. Had it not been for his brave service dog 'Chauncey,' his life would have been finished. Hansen told the Courier-Journal it was a miracle. He said: "She had been gone nearly two years and traveled hundreds of miles to find me. She had been lost and alone in city streets and placed in shelters only to survive by her determination and faith, driven to be together with me again."

"My God. That dog. That dog, Chauncey must have meant everything to him, his life…everything," she said in short breaths.

"Yep, talk around the town made tha' dog famous. Pooch would come in hereah at the library now and again and once that Dirck fella came into the history center hereah with the dog. But I was away for a spell durin' tha' time. People always said how sweet and lovin' tha' dog was. Always protectin' people."

"And you say they don't know what happened to her?"

Poindexter shook his head.

"Nope. Went somewhere to be cared for I suppose. Seem to rememba' there was some woman who might have taken it in. Maybe the town folk might know more."

Shannon looked through the remaining photographs. Her lead story on the history of Glenriver had now been forgotten. She looked up at the wall clock and frowned. It was 4:30 p.m. She had spent over four hours here. She wanted to continue but felt drained and still needed drive the fifty miles home to East Cabot and didn't like to travel in the dark. Even in good weather, the dark back roads were deceptive after sunset.

"I'll be back, Mr. Poindexter. This was so helpful. I'll be back."

She walked outside to the green and looked out. It was a late May day and the air had cooled to forty degrees yet it felt warm after the cold winter. The green sat on a hilltop that looked eastward towards Mount Moosilake and the rolling New Hampshire hills. The view was breathtaking. Large, stately elms surrounded the wide green lawn and at one end, there was a tall white flagpole displaying a worn American flag that fluttered in the breeze. The focal point of green was the impressive Congregational Church, which now sat, as the story was told, across the road from the north end of the common. Its familiarity drew her in.

The entire scene was straight from a Currier and Ives painting of a small quintessential Vermont village. It was as if time had receded a century. She closed her eyes and pictured it all in the silvery and shimmering daguerreotypes of yesterday.

Somewhere in the distance, a dog barked. She opened her eyes. Nobody was out this late afternoon. She looked out across the green towards the houses and fields beyond. She looked at the houses along the green and up Route 44. Judge Benson's house sat up there. Poindexter had said just four houses up, not far. Just four houses. She began to walk towards the house but something stopped her. What would she say if someone came out? Why would she be there?

She shouldn't be there.

She turned back to her car.

11

In the following weeks, Shannon's visits to Pownal, North Pownal, and Groton revealed fascinating historical records and she was close to finishing her first installment.

But it would have to wait. It was now mid-June and she was scheduled for a mandatory four-month visit with her cardiologists, Daniel Pratt and Christopher Davis. It would mean another trip to Boston, this time to the Women's Heart Health Program of the Massachusetts General in the city's Back Bay. The checkup would take two days and she arranged for a hotel near the facility. Her sister Brigid took off work for her. They arrived on a Tuesday afternoon. The checkup was scheduled for Wednesday afternoon.

Chauncey's hyperosmia had saved Sharon Farnum. A new CAT scan revealed a tiny shadow deep within her right breast. It had only been a few cells but the dog had found it. It was removed with a needle biopsy.

"Chauncey saved my life, Dru. I would have never gone for another scan had it not been for her. But her acute sense of smell worries me in other ways. I'm afraid she's overloaded with scents. She needs a diversion. Maybe you should now consider training her as a therapy dog like Callie. Her sweet nature and heightened sense of smell would be a great combination."

"I agree, but she's not ready. It's been over four months since Chauncey had run off up that mountain, and I still don't see much improvement. Something has gotten ahold of her. I don't know what."

"Her blood and urine tests are normal, and she looks and feels heathy, plenty of energy. The mixtures of smells everywhere might be throwing her off somehow."

"Her behavior worries me. She seems calm one minute but then becomes suddenly aroused. She's so familiar with all the smells and sounds here at CAS. There must be something outside of CAS that's drawing her. I just wish I knew what's going on in that brain of hers."

"I might be able to find out. I have a colleague in Boston who owes me a favor. Dr. Michael Terry, a neuroscientist studying dog behavior. He's been doing some remarkable things with MRI imaging. He trains the dogs to sit still in the MRI during a scan. He has them smell different objects and shows them pictures on a screen and can see which brain parts are active. It's a study on how a dog's brain functions. Groundbreaking stuff."

"Do you think she would take to doing that?"

"I'm certain. She's a smart girl and they train her for that. She'll probably love it."

Later that week, Sharon Farnum enrolled Chauncey in Dr. Terry's study at the Boston Center for MRI Imaging. Dru arranged for an overnight stay at Dr. Terry's home. He loved having the dogs and owners in his large house.

Chauncey was Dr. Terry's only client that week. They met him in a small room outside the MRI room.

"Dog brains are a lot more complex and sophisticated than we ever had imagined just few years ago. With her hyperosmia, I'm very interested in how Chauncey will respond to smell cues that we give her. And visual cues—they are tied in with smell. The first few days, we'll get her trained and acclimated to the scanner. She can't be sedated. She will have to stay awake and still while we scan her brain," Dr. Terry said.

"Good. She's trained to hand signals already. Hand up means a reward, a treat. Two hands horizontal, a blocking signal, no reward. I also have some items I brought with me for visual and smell signals," Dru said.

In the mock scanner, Chauncey learned to place her head onto a small wooden block and remain still. Treats were necessary but she learned quickly.

"Up!"

Chauncey climbed the five steps up the mock wooden scanner and rested her head onto the block, intently looking at Dru's hands.

"Stay!"

She remained motionless.

"Good girl!"

The scan would take thirty minutes during which she would remain still. The scanner would detect the blood flow through her brain, showing the active areas.

Then there were the loud MRI noises that could scare the dogs. Chauncey was trained to tolerate the noise by accepting headphones that would block out sounds. She given a treat each time the mock MRI noise sounded. Another day of training.

By the end of the week, she was able to climb up to the scanner with her headphones, place her head onto the block, and remain steady for at least 30 minutes.

The real MRI test was scheduled the next morning.

The MRI room was large, one that Chauncey had never seen. She walked in slowly, looking about the unfamiliar green cement walls and the large MRI machine, which sat up the familiar stairs. They fitted her with the headphones.

Dru was the only one in the room. She led Chauncey to the stairs. She spoke into a microphone so Chauncey could hear her. She raised her hand.

"Up!"

Chauncey climbed the stairs.

A treat.

Hands forward.

"Go in!"

Chauncey maneuvered herself to the edge of the MRI and put her head onto the platform.

"Good girl!"

Another treat.

Hands up.

"Stay!"

Dru moved to the other side of the scanner where she faced Chauncey through the large bore of the MRI.

Hands up.

"Stay."

She looked back to the control booth and gave Dr. Terry thumbs up to start the scan.

The large scanner began loud sound *THUMP THUMP*.

Chauncey remained steady.

Dr. Terry announced the tests.

"Ready for Test 1."

Dru's hand went up, signal for a treat.

THUMP THUMP THUMP.

"Test 2."

She shifted her hands horizontally—signal for no treat. The MRI sound continued.

THUMP THUMP.

"Test 3."

She opened a sealed bag and placed a shirt of hers towards Chauncey.

"Test 4."

She unsealed a bag with Dave's shirt and moved it close.

"Test 5."

Dru held up a picture of her smiling.

"Test 6."

Dave Ballard's smiling face.

"Tests 7 to 10."

Faces of the CAS trainers, some smiling, some angry and frowning.

"Good results. Let's keep going," Dr. Terry said.

The thumping continued as Dru held up a picture of CAS's training field, a photograph of another Golden Retriever, a photo of Callie. In between each, she showed Chauncey abstract grey images, nonsense images, meant to 'wash out' the last test.

A blank grey image was displayed.

Suddenly, Chauncey lifted her head and began to struggle inside the MRI tunnel.

Dr. Terry broke in.

"Stopping the scan. Something's happened."

The MRI stopped.

Chauncey scrambled to her feet and down the staircase. She ran for the door and scratched at it, whining.

Dru took off her headband and headphones. Chauncey squirmed about and began barking at her. Dru fixed her leash and let her out of the room.

"Maybe she has to relieve herself. She's upset about something," she said to Dr. Terry as they ran past the scanning booth.

Chauncey strained at the leash towards the building's back exit door, her nails sliding on the linoleum. She barked at the door.

Dru led her outside and removed the leash.

Chauncey ran through the lot to the building's front entrance, her nose to the ground, desperately trying to locate a scent.

She pawed at the fence that faced out to the building's entrance, barking and crying.

It took Dru nearly thirty minutes to get Chauncey back inside, where she collapsed on the cement floor of the control room.

A series of some thirty MRI images appeared on the large screen in front of them. Michael Terry pointed to the top row.

"We got some pretty typical results on the first scans here—treat, no treat, some of the smells. Look at this part of the brain. That's called the *caudate nucleus*—it's the C-shaped area right here. See the red and yellow area? That's a lot of blood flowing to that part, meaning the caudate was quite active. That brain part is active when there's a reward, similar to that in a human when a reward is signaled, like food or money. Her brain did all the right things. Lit up for a reward, and did not when you signaled no reward.

"Interesting. What's this here?" Dru said as she pointed to another row of images.

Caudate again. The smells of your shirt lit it up. So did the socks from Dave Ballard. Also, her caudate was active at the smiling faces of your staff. It tells us that she feels reward when she sees you or others she knows are happy. The frowning faces did not light up her caudate, no reward. Quite typical. Nothing out of the ordinary for dogs."

She pointed to the bottom images.

"What happened here? Really bright parts here."

"That's what baffles me. Never seen that much activity in any dog's brain before."

"Wow. Right here…that's brighter than all the other tests."

"This bright area is the *ventral tegmental*—the brain's reward circuit. It's a primitive nerve network that is active during great pleasure. Like love or longing."

"When was that triggered?"

"That's just after Test 9 before 10, the period when you held up a grey screen. That should be when the brain is quiet. But that was exactly when Chauncey's tegmental area flooded with blood!"

He pointed to the image time stamp. It read *1:43 p.m.*

"Yes, that coincided with her moving around. She wasn't dreaming," Dru said.

"No, she was awake. We see that here, cortex activity is normal, meaning she wasn't asleep. Something really aroused her tegmental area, the pleasure or longing part. But there was no image stimulus then."

"Could it have been from a smell? Is the room sealed off?"

"Yes, it's normally impossible for dogs to smell anything in the MRI facility. It's sealed. But we have tested for that in the past. But you told us about Chauncey's hyperosmia, her acute smelling ability. It's possible she was able to smell something outside of the facility. That would be very rate and I've never seen that."

"She's been bothered by something. She seems upset and I can only think it's smells that arouse her."

"And it's curious that the most activity was centered in that area of her brain active during intense love and longing."

They looked down at Chauncey who was resting her head on her paws. She looked up at them with a look of sorrow and defeat. It was the look she gave Dru the day Dirck had died. She just never seemed to relax, always appearing to be longing for something but never able find it.

Chauncey snorted and closed her eyes.

Shannon was late for her medical appointment. It was scheduled for 2 p.m. today but because it was a warm sunny day, she decided to walk to the Women's Heart Health building.

In the last block, she passed the Boston Center for MRI Imaging.

A sensation swept over her.

She stopped in front of the building and cupped her hands to look through the glass door.

Inside, the wall clock blinked *1:43 p.m.*

12

Shannon's stories were taking longer to write. And Bud thought the first one lacked its usual sharpness. Still, she pushed forward with new visits to Pownal, North Pownal, and Groton, towns further north from Glenriver. Despite more visits to town offices and libraries and talks with the locals, her interest grew flat.

Inside the Groton, Vermont village office she approached town manager.

"How far is Glenriver from here?"

"Not far, 'bout thirty minutes just down route 4A to Pownal way, then ova' on old Route 44 into the town."

Her story was only an outline at this point and the deadline was in two days, but she wanted to get over to Glenriver instead. She jammed her notes into the briefcase and left.

When she turned left onto Route 44, it was nearly 6 p.m. and sun had just set behind Mount Moosilake. She drove along the familiar green and town library where she had met John Poindexter only a week earlier.

She spotted Sarah Bristoll pushing a wheelbarrow along her driveway and pulled in.

"Hello Mrs. Bristoll. Do you remember me? Shannon Murphy from East Cabot."

Sarah took off her gloves and extended her hand.

"Yep, rememba' you. It's Miss Bristol."

"Oh, sorry. Hate to disturb your gardening, but wanted to ask you about your neighbor at the old Judge Benson's house."

Sarah's brow furled.

"Why you ask?"

Shannon hesitated.

"We'll, I was doing some research on Glenriver and ran across the story about the man who lived there with his dog. I was wondering about them."

The woman was only five feet and she stared up at Shannon, her steel blue eyes uninviting.

"Tha' story's a recent one. Not much about Glenriver history theyah. Not surah why you need to know this."

Shannon regretted asking.

"Well, I guess it's not of historic significance. But understand the man who lived there had a father, who was important figure in the town. A Douglas G. Hansen, a Major in the army."

Sarah's face relaxed.

"Oh yes, Douglas. Knew tha' nice man long ago. He passed when his son lived here. Can't rememba' the year."

Shannon looked over at the homestead.

"Does anyone live there now?"

"No, don't believe so. Been empty for some months. Don't know who owns the place now. That son, he passed away theyah. Miss seein' him now and then. Nice fella."

"He died in that house? When was that?

"Months ago, last fall, I believe. Well, they took him away in ambulance. Not surah if he died theyah, to be certain. Lived there with tha' dog of his."

Sarah pointed at the stone wall.

"His back field and mine are separate only from my low handmade stone wall. Used to see him and his pretty dog out in tha' yard many times. Even in the dead of winter. That dog really protected him. Met the pooch a couple of times. Sweet dog, friendly, always wagging that big bushy tail of hers."

Shannon's heart quickened. She leaned forward.

"You okay, Miss? You need some watah?"

Sarah turned back to her house and brought them both a glass of ice water.

"You think anyone would mind if I just walked over in the back of the placc. Just to take a quick peek in the back. That field looks so lovely."

"Well no, nobody theyah. You can go up around the front and into the back. My stone wall's delicate."

Shannon thanked her and walked around the gravel sidewalk to the homestead front. It was now twilight and distances were deceptive. As she approached the front of the homestead, John Poindexter's historic photographs came into view. The place stood back off the road almost hidden amongst the trees. The long driveway was lined with brilliant white birches, just like in the old copper images.

The house sat slightly up on a small hill. The frame-and-clapboard front was distinguished from others by its handsome, enclosed entrance porch projecting from the center of the five-bay façade. The large black front door was flanked by louvered side panels and capped by a handsome elliptical louvered fan. All of it hand-crafted nearly 200 years earlier. The top granite step was adorned with the original iron boot mud scrapers. The effect was spectacular.

She walked further down the driveway along the side of handsome house. She closed her eyes and pictured a man sitting in front of a large fire, his dog by his side, looking up at him in the large room. She opened her eyes. The home was dark and empty.

She walked out into the sprawling back yard that looked out to the wide eight-acre field. A gentle evening breeze wafted by her, its smells sweet, familiar. Her heart fluttered.

She went to the stone wall that separated the house from Sarah Bristoll's place. At one edge, she noticed a small mound grown over with moss. She scraped moss and dirt away to reveal the edge of something. It was a jagged bone filled with dirt. She pulled it out and brought it to her nose. It was pungent. It must have belonged the dog, that dog *Chauncey*. She reburied it in reverence and sat onto the dirt and rested her head onto her knees.

In the shadows, she fell asleep. At least she thought she did.

She raised her head and looked at her watch. Eight o'clock. Deep purple shadows surrounded her. In the last light, on one side of the driveway she looked at silhouette of the far-off garage barn. One of its small doors was open and, in the darkness, she could just make out the outline of a dog, its bushy tail swinging lightly. She squinted her eyes closed and reopened them. The dog was still there, motionless, staring at her across the expanse.

She walked further out to the field and looked out. A pale moon shown through the thin clouds, casting a dim light across the field. She could barely see across it.

A gentle wind drew past her and in it, came a whisper.

How many times have we stood here and looked out at the field together?

How many times have we counted the deer in the field from here?

She looked around. She was alone.

"What do you want of me?" she said to the empty dark space.

Remember how we used to share this all, all that we had here?

I miss you so, my dear friend, all that we shared!

"Yes…yes, I feel that too. I miss…what we shared," she repeated to the mysterious darkness. She looked back towards the dark barn but the dog was now gone.

She felt faint and thought to leave.

As she walked by the house, she peered into a window. From the far end of the large room, a stray light dimly lit the room, a night light, perhaps, maybe an odd reflection. It took a minute for her to make sense of it. She traced the walls and the mantle and fireplace, along the lone couch and the rooms beyond.

In the distance, something moved, a shadow across one door to the next, something moving slowly beyond, a figure in the dark.

I'm here. Here with you. Close.

In the darkness about her, images came to her, images seen by a baby, a toddler, a young woman, an adult, all the images rushing to her at once. Standing over an innocent white puppy, unable to touch it, a father in blind rage waving his arms about, a mother weeping in desperation.

Then, a man appeared before her. He was dressed in a dark-green officer's uniform with gold bars. He smiled broadly.

She's yours now. Find her. Protect her.

Shannon ran back towards the field. The clouds had parted and moonlight lit the yard.

Then she saw the dog, the same dog. It stood in the center of the field, a golden image glowing in the moonstruck field like a statue, frozen in a brilliant stance, its back legs cocked, its feathers floating in the breeze. Its gaze was fixed on her.

Her heart pounded.

She raised her arm but it didn't move.

Just come, she whispered, *please, come to me.*

She raised her hand higher and waited.

The clouds folded back across the summer moon and it was all gone.

13

It was as if Chauncey had returned to Dirck's grave. Again and again, she slid back into the things that sapped her, drew her away. Day after day, as she lay in half slumber, she pictured his casket being lowered into the ground. She still dreamed that she slept beside his chair, woke to him, walked with him in the autumn woods and winter's snows.

She had no rest.

"The trip for the brain scan made her worse, Dave. I can't understand what happened there."

Dru had been back at CAS for a week and Chauncey had fallen back into a worsening depression that scared her.

"I need to get Dr. Farnum back. She might bring some new perspective."

"I think it's time to give her a job. I remember when she came back from that prison program at the beginning of her time here and how her training helped bring her confidence back."

"Like a therapy dog?"

"Train her like Callie, Dru. I think she'd be perfect in a hospital or hospice setting."

"I hope she's up for that."

"I got Callie through it and she had no training. Chauncey had been a brilliant service dog and she'll make a great therapy dog."

"You're right, Dave. She's such a special girl. I just want to do the right thing for her."

But they first had to get Chauncey back mentally. They began taking her on longer hikes, running her along the kennel grounds, stimulating her with play from other dogs, and every morning, the training staff interacted with her, praising her for even the smallest feats. And she was put back on a high-level protein diet. She slept, ate, and ran with Callie.

By summer, Chauncey's mood improved noticeably. She happily greeted everyone who came to visit. She was taught the basics of how to interact with people who didn't respond to her, who would be angry with her or push her away, the sick and depressed people she would have to comfort.

Then came the facility visits. The goal was to visit different facilities each week, sometimes two each week, and on each trip, she would visit two patients. Her training would build up to 100 patient-visits, as the therapy certification required.

Her first visit was to a local nursing home, the Ponds Place in Baker's Mills. She arrived with Callie who had another assignment with Dave.

Chauncey's first patient was Mrs. Beatrice Terrance, a ninety-three-year-old woman who had recently lost her husband of sixty-five years to an agonizing cancer death. The woman was angry and depressed, confined to a wheelchair.

Dru led in Chauncey while the coordinator watched.

"Mrs. Terrance. We have a special treat for you this morning. A lovely dog," a nurse said.

The old woman looked away.

"Don't want a damned dog," she mumbled.

"No, it's not for you, just for a visit."

"Don't want it. Go away."

Dru stood away from the woman while Chauncey quietly sat by her side. She didn't like the smells that swirled in her nose.

"Bring her over," said the nurse quietly.

Dru led Chauncey to the woman and signaled for her to sit next to her wheelchair. The woman looked down at the obedient dog staring up at her.

"This is Chauncey. She's a Golden Retriever that used to be a veteran's service dog."

There was silence as the woman considered the dog.

Dru gave Chauncey a command and she put her muzzle on the woman's knee in a gesture of friendship. The woman pushed her away.

"Don't want…a dog."

Chauncey was used to rejection. Her penetrating amber eyes stared steadily at Mrs. Terrance. The woman's eyes began to flutter. She reached down.

"Okay. Okay, come here, girl," said the old woman softly.

Chauncey gently placed her paw on the wheelchair and rose up and licked Mrs. Terrance's face. The woman put her arm around the dog and leaned into her.

"You're a good girl. You bring people love," she whispered into the dog's ear.

Chauncey gave the woman another swipe of her tongue and jumped down and let out a low whine, a sweet sound. The woman smiled.

The nursing staff had not seen Mrs. Terrance smile since she had been brought in two months ago.

"We'll bring her around for visits if you wish," said the nurse.

"Good. I want to see this sweet girl again. She likes me."

She reached down for Chauncey who moved her muzzle onto her lap.

"You be a good girl while I'm gone from you. No hanky-panky, okay?"

Chauncey let out a short bark in response.

By every measure, the visit had been a success. They had brought two other dogs to Mrs. Terrance without luck yet Chauncey was able to break through the woman's crippling depression and anger enough to keep her going.

For over thirty years, Dru had seen this with her broken soldiers but was still amazed how her dog could break through someone so depressed like Mrs. Terrance. This was just as powerful.

"Dave, this will be Chauncey's new life. She's perfect for this!"

"I knew she'd be a star, but we've got a long way to go to get her certified. Just ninety patients-visits more."

But they went quickly. In just eight weeks, Chauncey had visited over thirty-three facilities with three patients each, some at nursing homes, others at hospitals, for one-hundred patient-visits.

Through all of it, she passed with distinction, earning her the prestigious status of a combined service and therapy dog. Many of her patients had lost hope and wanted to die. Chauncey found a way through their grief and unending weight of looming death to give them some faith and promise in life, even for the short time she would spend with them. Sometimes, she could smell their disease, fear, and despair, but it only drew her to them more. It gave her strength to help them like she had for years with Dirck.

By the end of her training, Chauncey became known as *The Golden Angel* and was in great demand by her patients. On the last visit, the therapy trainer met with Dru to sign her certification.

"Chauncey is natural. Now, the real test begins. We want to see how she'll do with the children and their grief-stricken parents. Those are the most difficult patients. Therapy dogs have mixed results with the kids. We need to put Chauncey into that world."

The following week, that assignment came at the well-known Saint Jude's Children's Hospital in New York City. Pediatric patients from all over the United States, even some from overseas, came to the top-ranked pediatric facility that took in children with developmental disorders, cancers, and fatal genetic diseases. For the babies and toddlers, death had little meaning, but many patients were school children who understood that sickness and death were real and fear of the unknown terrified them.

The parents were especially difficult to reach. They were paralyzed with fear turned inward as depression, and even experienced nurses and physicians found it difficult to deal with their emotions. Suicide among parents was common. It was the most demanding task for any therapy dog.

The first day, Chauncey was introduced to the staff of Saint Jude's oncology ward with three other dogs: "Lulu," a smart standard poodle, "Moose," a handsome black Newfoundland, and "Zoe," a quick and smart Jack Russell Terrier. Dru found the mix odd. How could a tough little terrier calm the fears of a dying child? But they all had been proven and certified as therapy dogs, some for years. Chauncey had been certified for only a month.

Chauncey was paired with eight-year-old girl, Jessie, who suffered from cancer that had spread to her brain. The child could barely speak and was partially blind. But her mind was still intact and she often would ramble on about whatever her disordered brain told her. When she had turned six, her parents had bought her a rescue puppy, a mixed breed, and it lifted the child's spirits but after only five months, the puppy developed a rare liver disease and had to be put down. The loss paralyzed the sick child even more. Her parents dared not buy the girl another dog and neighbors would bring their own cats and dogs, once even a parakeet, to cheer the child. All without success.

Earlier that week, Jessie and her parents had driven over twenty hours from Kansas for care at Saint Jude, but after only a day reviewing her tests, a team of pediatric oncologists found the cancer was untreatable and had given the young girl only one month more of life.

While Chauncey waited in the nursing station, Dru was brought into Jessie's room to meet the parents and, on that day, two evaluators from the canine therapy program. They all stood by the large bed where the girl lay engulfed in bed warmers, a feeding tube, and wires snaking about the small girl.

The evaluators would observe how Chauncey would react to the girl during the thirty-minute session, making note of changes in Jessie's mood during and after the dog's exit. While the dog interacted with Jessie, conversation would be halted, allowing a bond to form between them. Dru told the parents and Jessie about Chauncey, that she had been a wonderful service dog for a veteran and had recently become known as *The Golden Angel* during her training.

They were anxious to meet her.

Dru went to the hallway to get Chauncey who was enjoying a moment with the nurses, all of them kneeling to her, cooing after her. She had just been groomed that week and her feathers were velvet. She reached down and held Chauncey's head.

"Ok, girl, we're ready. This is your moment. You get to meet little Jessie. She's not well and will die. I need you to help her, help her parents."

Chauncey looked up with her gentle warm eyes, signaling that she was ready and anxious to help. Dru led her into the child's room. Everyone sat back away from the girl's bedside. Trainers had placed a ramp next to the bed. They walked to the ramp. Chauncey stared up at the girl.

"Hello Jessie. This is Chauncey. She's come to visit you for a while," said Dru.

She backed away from the bed.

Jessie tilted her head towards Chauncey. A moment passed with no reaction. Then the girl moved closer to get a better look. Chauncey sat quietly, her eyes fixed on the small child. A foul odor filled her nose. She knew the young girl was very sick.

The girl's small hand reached out towards the dog. Chauncey gently crawled part way up the ramp and stretched her head to the child. The girl leaned to one side and brought her hand to the dog's muzzle. Chauncey's tongue gently swiped across Jessie's hand.

She smiled.

"She likes me," Jessie said.

The parents smiled through their tears.

"She does like you, honey," sobbed the mother.

The father couldn't speak.

Chauncey climbed carefully up onto the girl's bed and laid next to her, burying her head in the girl's arm. The dog's weight soothed the child and she closed her eyes. The two laid together in silence as the girl smoothed her hand across the dog's head and feathery coat. Chauncey leaned up and licked the girl's face.

Jessie giggled.

Only muffled sobs could be heard.

"Our girl just gives that feeling that *everything is okay and good—just focus on me and I'll make it okay*," whispered Dru to one trainer who had begun to cry.

In the thirty silent minutes that followed, the stress and grief and hopelessness that had filled the room had been replaced with calmness and joy. With love.

Chauncey had given Jessie the gift of joy in the wake of impending death. The effect was terrific.

At the conclusion of the visit, it was difficult untangling child and dog, and as Chauncey was led down the ramp and to the door, the girl sat up to watch her.

"Bring her back! I want her! I want Chauncey," Jessie said in her loud child's voice.

It was the first time Jessie had spoken in months. She sounded full of life.

"We will, Jessie. We'll come and visit again soon. Very soon," said Dru.

But Chauncey would not return.

A month later, Jessie died in her parent's arms.

Chauncey passed through every evaluation with distinction, and the staff constantly sought her for more visits with even the most difficult young patients.

From online postings from parents, thousands of people saw pictures of the beautiful dog with her patients and began asking for the *Golden Angel* to visit their own child.

At the New York Children's Hospital, Chauncey visited Evan, a four-year-old dying boy with pancreatic cancer and his parents. There was then a visit to the twelve-year-old twins conjoined at the chest, Kellie and Kalie, with their adopted parents Mr. and Mrs. Bowden. The hour-long visits brought them all joy, comfort they had not felt in years.

When she would return to a facility, it was sometimes difficult for Chauncey to discover that a child was now gone, for she remembered them all. Yet her work displaced her own grief from the loss of Dirck, and by that September, she had gained back her confidence.

The smells that had pulled her away seemed to have faded and she felt more relaxed and directed.

Dru finally could see a change in her dog.

Yet a small, nearly imperceptible memory lingered within her, the painful buried memory of Dirck.

It had not disappeared.

14

Shannon almost missed the small advertisement. She normally didn't read them, but sometimes there were hidden gems in the *Caledonian Record.* And this one was short enough to get her attention. She read it a second time.

Four-bedroom historic home in Central Vermont. Spacious grounds, beautiful views. $2,000. 802-783-3983.

It was the familiar *802* Vermont exchange.

She dialed the number.

"This is Dru."

"Hello, I am inquiring about your rental. Is this the right number?"

"Yes, it is. What questions can I answer?"

"Where is the rental located?"

"It's in central Vermont, up near Groton and North Pownal. Out in the country."

"And it's historic?"

"Yes, over 200 years old."

"I would love to see it."

"Would this be only for you? It's a big place, two stories. Several bedrooms."

"Yes, just me. I'm single but employed and can provide references."

"Well, you best see the place first. I can meet you there later this week, even on the weekend might be better for me."

"You name the time, and I'll meet you there. My name's Shannon. Shannon Murphy."

"I am Dru Vaughn. I'm in upstate New York but not terribly far. How about this Saturday at 1 p.m.? Would that work?"

"Surely. Thank you."

Shannon hadn't been seeking a new place to live but in the past weeks, she had been increasingly drawn to that part of Vermont and had spent more time there.

That Saturday brought rain to the region and the day was dark, and it was difficult to see landmarks. She set her phone to the coordinates that Dru had sent her. The map took her on an unfamiliar and unmarked back road along the beautiful Vermont countryside. She passed a large school and as the checkered flag appeared on the phone, she slowed. *You have reached your destination* said the GPS.

She stopped and looked to her right. There was no house there, only a wide meadow that looked across a valley. It seemed like she had been here before. On her left, a large bush maple tree obscured the view. She inched forward.

Then the house came into view. She slammed on the breaks.

The address on the mailbox read *3982*.

This was the Judge Benson's home in Glenriver! She looked again. She couldn't believe this was for rent!

She pulled into the familiar driveway. The house looked smaller, somehow more inviting.

A woman walked out onto the stone patio to greet her. She was older with greying hair and was fit. She had a kind face. Shannon extended her hand.

"Hello, I'm Shannon Murphy."

Her bright smile is the first thing Dru noticed. She appeared kind and sincere, a woman of substance.

"Good to meet you, I'm Dru. Let me show you around. First, you can see how beautiful the setting is here. These old trees really frame the lovely grounds and that large field beyond. It's owned by the town, so nobody can build on it. It's yours to use for hiking if you prefer."

Shannon looked out at the familiar landscape. It still took her breath away.

As they walked into the house, Shannon hesitated. She had often tried to imagine how the house looked like inside.

They walked into the kitchen. It was a simple 'country kitchen' as many locals called it—no frills, well laid out with plenty of counter space. It was warm and inviting. Immensely charming.

"Nice kitchen to cook in, plenty of room. The previous owner enjoyed the morning views from here."

"Previous owner? Who was that?" Dru said. But she knew who it was.

Dru frowned.

"They are no longer here. Why do you ask?"

"Was it that soldier? The one they wrote about in the paper, that *Glenriver Courier Journal*?"

She stared at Shannon and frowned.

"Yes, he was a veteran. But he's no longer here. I'm not sure why you need…."

"I'm sorry. I just read about him and his dog saving him. I am a reporter for a paper in East Cabot, and had seen the story in the library's historical society. Was just curious."

Her questions had stopped the tour. Dru was unsure if she was the right person to rent the house.

"Well, I'm the owner of the property now and we need someone here who is quiet and respectful of this old home. The neighbors are mostly long-term residents and, well, pretty quiet. They don't gossip much."

"I apologize. I guess it's my nature to be curious about the history of a place. It's such an interesting home, and I am quite aware of its storied history with Judge Benson. I think it's quite beautiful."

That seemed to work. Dru smiled and led her into the large living room.

"This is one of two great rooms, each with their own large Rumford fireplaces, both working. This bay window looks out north towards the back and into the Glenriver Town Forest. The rooms have wonderful light from the north and south from the New Hampshire mountains. And it's very quiet here."

Shannon was looking about but her attention was drawn down to the leather couch in the center of the room. She slowly walked towards it. Stuck in one seam of the couch was a tuft of blonde hair. She nonchalantly leaned down and pulled it free as Dru faced the other direction.

"Of course, it's all furnished but please don't rearrange anything. It's kept as we want it."

Shannon wasn't sure who the "we" were. The house belonged to Dru. Perhaps she had a partner.

"And here is the first bedroom and adjoining large bathroom with original wood paneling."

Shannon swirled the tuft of hair in her fingers as she watched the woman move from window to window, adjusting the drapes. The afternoon sun brightly lit Dru's face. The woman looked familiar, like someone she had once known. She appeared kind and strong, yet sympathetic and emotional.

"Have we ever met, Dru?"

She gave Shannon an odd look.

"I don't think so. Where would we have met?"

She realized she was raising more suspicion.

"Oh, you just look like someone I once knew, I'm sorry."

The tour continued.

"This is not set up as a bedroom now. More of an office."

There was a small desk in the corner and a single chair tucked into it. A bookcase sat on the opposite wall, still filled with books but all the photographs had been removed. Simple black-and-white chintz drapes hung from three double-hung windows. The rest of the room was unadorned. Its simplicity was alluring.

Shannon nonchalantly brought the tuft of fur to her nose. It had had a faint smell. She closed her eyes. Warmth flooded her.

"Are you okay?"

"Oh, yes, I guess I'm just taking this all in. It's so beautiful and charming here."

"Let's go upstairs then."

At the top of the narrow staircase was a landing leading to other rooms. To her left was a small bedroom and across the landing was a bathroom and a larger bedroom. From the landing, a narrow entrance led down into the master bedroom four feet below. The stepped through the narrow entry way.

"Watch your head. It's deceptively low. The previous owner sometimes forgot and hit his head on the overhang."

Shannon imagined the veteran crouched down on the small staircase, rubbing his head, the Golden licking his face in consolation. She squeezed the tuft in her hand.

"This room is wonderful. In the early days, it was a dormitory for boys who attended the Glenriver Academy, which sits just beyond those woods out there," Dru said as she pointed out a large 24-light window that looked out to the back yard and field beyond.

Dru walked about the room, pointed to the windows.

"Up here, the room is full of light. There are seven low double-hung windows throughout the room."

A large stripped bed faced the large picture window. Shannon moved to its side and smoothed her hand across the mattress. She tried to imagine the man lying here in bed, his dog next to him, as they lazily stared out to the field, anticipating that morning's hikes.

"And the bathroom is out through the entrance in a small dormer room. Quite convenient. But I imagine you'd want to make your bedroom downstairs."

"Oh no! This is where I should be, up here with this view. It has such a feeling. I can't describe it."

"Yes, it's always been a strong point of the home, especially with its history," Dru said.

"It's history? You man the boys' dormitory?"

"Yes, many wonderful stories from some of the residents who remembered it from their parents. Quite a rambunctious place filled with boys who would become men, men who would change the history of this town."

"Really? That most interests me. I am writing pieces for the *Caledonian Record* about Vermont's history, some unusual untold stories. I would very much like more on history of this place."

"That's best gotten through John Poindexter just down the road at the Historical Society. It's inside the library just on the town green. You should meet him. He's full of stories."

"Yes, I have already. He was most helpful. I got to see some of the old photographs of this place taken back when Judge Benson lived here. That was back when a gated fence surrounded the house and cows roamed the fields."

"Yes, but that was before this part of the house was built. The dorm here was opened in the 1930s."

She tried to imagine the room at that time, its old worn wooden floors and scuff marks along the walls from rambunctious boys and stained ceilings from roof leaks.

Shannon turned to leave and noticed a small photograph sitting on a table in back of the bed. She walked to it and leaned forward.

"Oh, I'm sorry, that's not supposed to be here. We tried to empty the house of the previous occupant's belongings."

Shannon stared at the small picture. Framed in tarnished silver was a 3x5 color photograph of Dirck and Chauncey, taken just the year before. Dirck was sitting in the leather sofa in the great room facing the camera. He was not smiling. The dog was sprawled across Dirck, staring up at him. Dru had taken the photograph, one of the few of Dirck in his later years when he had grown sicker and didn't want any photographs made. But he had agreed to this one. The image was captivating. She couldn't take her eyes off it.

She reached around Shannon and picked up the frame and tucked it into her vest.

"What? I mean, where did that beautiful dog go? Is she still with us?"

It seemed like an innocent question.

Dru cocked her head.

"The dog is quite well. Why do you ask?"

She bunched the tuft of hair into her palm.

"No reason. She just looks happy. I just wanted to know if she's still...."

"She's fine. Let's go back through to the landing and I'll show you the rest of the second floor."

They continued walking through the second story, the bedrooms, the bathroom. Shannon traced the angles of the floor, imagining the dog racing through the many spaces, up and down the stairs of the house, the place that would soon be her home.

"Well, that's the inside tour. Let's go in the back and I'll show you the yard."

"No, it's okay, I've seen it…I mean I saw it from the windows. It's quite large."

"Well, I can give you some time to think about it."

"I don't need time. I very much want to live here, Dru."

"Okay, but I will need three references and employment details. You can send them by email or regular mail if you wish."

That week, Dru received letters from Bud, Brigid, and Sherry, a long-time editor at the *Caledonian Record.* The letters spoke of Shannon's loyalty, her steadfast and reliable nature, her kindness. Included were articles she had written, her hire letter from Bud dated some sixteen years earlier, a recent photograph of her. It impressed Dru and that week, a one-year lease arrived at her East Cabot apartment.

She explained to Bud that she needed a more inspiring place to write and that she'd be down once a week to go over the pieces with him. The deal was sealed and that week, her old apartment was closed down. Brigid helped her sister move.

The following week, the sisters arrived at the Judge Benson's homestead. Late-summer white pom-pom flowers from the large Limelight hydrangeas drooped across the entryway. An empty bird's nest was perched over the entry porch light and on the large front door hung a welcome huckleberry-primrose wreath.

"Shannon! This is charming. I'll have to visit a lot!"

"I hope you will. It's all so…new."

But as Shannon stepped across the threshold, a sense of familiarity filled her. The heavy granite steps, the solid heavy black door, the arched entryway, the interior walls and planked floors, the large fireplaces, all seemed intimate. It was as if she were moving back into a home she had lived in for many years. She felt emotional, sentimental really, a wistful nostalgia for a former time, like a homeland she had always longed for, but these feelings were foreign, for her youth had been filled with sorrow and fear and life in drab, empty rooms. Yet the sentiment here felt true. But she also sensed mystery. She wanted to immerse herself in the familiar but was afraid that the house would reveal the secrets it held.

"You sure have a lot of stuff from that small apartment. Hard to believe you have these many boxes," said Brigid.

"A lot of this is books and papers. I'll have plenty of room to put it all. Let's get all this settled."

It was early evening by the time all the essentials were unpacked and boxes were in their proper rooms, each labeled with *Upstairs bathroom* or *Lower bedroom* or *Great Room #1*.

The sisters sat on the sofa, exhausted.

Shannon fished her hand around in the corners of pads, hoping to find another tuft of hair.

"I wonder who had lived here. Do you know of its history?"

"Some of it. A man had owned it just before he passed away. He was a war veteran named Dirck Hansen and he had a Golden Retriever service dog. A girl dog called *Chauncey*. I've seen pictures of him and his dog. I don't know what happened to her."

"How did you know their names?"

"It was written up in the *Glenriver Journal*. How his dog saved him. It's an incredible story. Do you want to hear it?"

"Oh, well, not now. But at least you don't have to worry about a dog. Just you and your writing. It'll be inspiring to sit in that office looking out to the mountains each morning with your tea."

Shannon stared into the black fireplace. She turned to Brigid.

"You know, it would be so comforting to have a dog here. Right here. Just to know it's here to help."

Brigid frowned.

"Why would you want a dog to have to take care of Shan'? That's a lot of work and expense."

"But it would be comforting."

Brigid looked at her sister. Shannon's eyes had begun to tear up. She reached out and took her hand.

"Hey Shan'. This is a joyful day—you have a wonderful place—let's take a walk around."

As Shannon walked through the rooms, each turn and corner of house felt more and more familiar. They walked down to the basement.

"I didn't see this on the tour."

It was dim, the only light coming from the small hopper windows facing west and east. An abandoned water tank and cistern sat in the center of the room, and on the other side was a rusty oil tank. The space smelled musty and old. She looked down at rough concrete floor. There was a rust-colored stain where she stood. It had been on this spot that Dirck Hansen had lain bleeding and near death before his dog had found him years earlier, saving him from murderous thieves.

She felt a chill.

They went outside to the spacious yard. The lawn looked like a manicured golf course, its freshly mowed rows of light and dark green strips fanning out towards the large field beyond. It was summer and the large meadow was filled with purple and yellow wildflowers. Beyond was the town forest.

Shannon looked at the field and noticed a young fawn hopping awkwardly towards its mother who watched her baby from the forest's edge. She remembered the voice she had heard:

How many times have we stood here and looked out at the field…

how many times have we counted the deer in the field?

A breeze whistled through the evergreens. She closed her eyes. In the distance, a dog barked. She cocked her head. Another bark. It came from her right.

They walked to the edge of Sarah Bristoll's yard. Across the expanse, two or three houses away, Shannon spotted a large black and tan and white dog lumbering about in a fenced yard, disturbed by something, barking into the warm air. Probably riled up from them, the newcomers.

She laughed.

"Look at that!"

Brigid was facing back at the house. She turned.

"What? What do you see?"

"That dog! Look at him. Probably a Bernese."

"A what?"

"A Bernese Mountain Dog! He's beautiful. Just look at him!"

"How do you know it's a 'him'?"

"Oh, that's a boy all right. Handsome fellow. I'll have to meet him now that I'm here."

Brigid frowned and shook her head.

"Okay, whatever."

The rest of the day was filled with unpacking, hiking, and eating from the local food wagon, *Sweet's Wicked Awesome Barbeque.* Falling-off-the-bone short ribs dripping with sweet sauce, biscuits big enough for three, freshly picked corn-on-the-cob, slaw smothered in creamy mayonnaise, onions and peppers. Wicked all right. It wasn't on the diet, but perfect for her first day as a treat, a taste of Glenriver, Vermont.

That first night, Brigid slept downstairs and Shannon retired to the large upstairs bedroom. She lay between the fresh sheets without blankets, the windows open to the cool summer breeze that blew across the bed. It was dark, darker than she could remember.

As slumber overtook her, she again saw a vision. A golden dog was running towards her in the field, its smooth hair floating in the wind, a sheer surging of beauty, each separate muscle and joint and sinew aglow and rampant, expressing itself in perfect movement, flying at her exuberantly under a blanket of stars.

She sat up, her heart racing. She jumped out of bed to the window and looked out. It was pitch black.

"Where are you?" she spoke to the close darkness. "What do you want?"

From the tops of the spruce trees, winds whispered through the windows. It seemed to be urging her *close…closessss.* She lay by one low window, her head on its sill, deeply breathing the sweet night air, listening to the subdued and sleepy murmurs of the forest through the night in a reverie, her heart aloft.

A shaft of sunlight shot through the trees and into the window, waking her. She rose and looked out. How different the morning looked! Light flooded the large field, ready for its creatures to awaken into the land's welcoming warm arms.

The sisters compared their nights, had breakfast, and took a long walk around the flowering meadow.

By mid-morning, Shannon was alone in the large house. She made six trips up and down carrying boxes, pictures, handfuls of hangers. She felt grateful that she could climb stairs again.

She rested in the back room of the house, the place Dru had called 'the sunroom.' A small screen porch sat off it, its doors open, ushering in warm mid-day breezes. She lay on the couch looking at the light blue hydrangeas that lined the back of the house.

The silence was punctuated by a far-off bark. Then another. The neighbor's dog again. She ran out to the back of the property and looked across the expanse. The big dog lumbered about the enclosure, barking into the afternoon air. Sarah Bristoll was next door in her garden.

"Hello Sarah. Miss Bristoll. It's Shannon Murphy."

Sarah unsteadily climbed to her feet and looked at her oddly.

"Wha' you doin' here? Oh, I see—are you the one that rented the old place? Heard 'bout that. Wonderful to have someone there. Glad it's you!"

"Mind if I cross over? I didn't want to impose."

"That's fine, just step gently over my wall. Careful not to dislodge any loose stones."

The two women walked through the Bristoll property. The field was a large orchard filled with Wolf River apple trees, some over eighty years old. The canopy of deep green was filled with hundreds of plump apples displaying their first red glow.

"Don't eat them much anymore. For the deer now. They love those sweet apples. You'll see them out here in the evening havin' their dinner. Dozens of them even with their young'uns. I love to sit out here on my porch and sip my sherry and watch them enjoying the fruit. Warms my heart a bunch."

"Whose dog is that two houses down from here in the large fenced yard?"

"Don't rightly know. Some man and his daughter who moved here 'bout a year or so now. She goes to the Academy. Nice girl. Father's odd, though. Pretty dog."

"I wonder if they would mind if I went to visit."

"I don't think so. Dog's a friendly sort. They keep him penned up there. Too much danga' for a dog loose on its own out here."

"I'll be sure to come back to visit if you need anything, let me know, Miss Bristol."

"Oh child, call me Sarah and I'm fine but if I can help you in any way, let me know. I'm not good for much 'cept this gardening. At my age, it's all I can do. I'm pushin' ninety-two next year."

Sarah went back to her garden, bending and twisting about with ease. Shannon shook her head, amazed at how easily the woman could move. *Gardening is therapy* she thought.

She walked across the field to the large fenced pen. The dog was bellowing in exuberance at her. She crouched to him.

"Hello big fellow. Aren't you a handsome boy?"

She carefully placed her hand between the fence posts. The dog licked her, his warm wet tongue filling her hand. The dog's black face was wide with a white stripe that ran along his muzzle and up between his eyes, which were handsomely framed with brushes of rust. He was mostly black except for a thick white ruff in the shape of a broad cross on his chest. The dog's bushy tail swung powerfully as he shoved his muzzle through the fence to get more of her hand.

"Hello?" a young voice echoed across the field.

"Hello. Hope you don't mind me petting your beautiful dog," Shannon said in the direction of the voice.

There was no answer and she couldn't see anyone. A girl came bounding down the back stairs.

"Oh Barney, are you bothering someone again? Who's out there?" the girl said.

"He's not bothering me. I was just wanted to pet him."

"Hi. I'm Joannie. And this is Barney Boy. He's ours. Really just a big baby."

She could tell the girl was more of young woman of seventeen, perhaps, although it was difficult to say from her plain dress and lack of makeup. Her face was unremarkable but pleasant and clean. She had a slight overbite and a small pug nose, giving her the appearance of a younger girl, but her unchecked shapely figure was not that of a young girl. She seemed unaware of her distinct femininity. Her brown hair was pulled back into a ponytail that bobbed around as she jerked enthusiastically about.

Somehow, the girl looked familiar.

"We moved here a year and a half ago, dad and I. He's in the house right now. Who are you?

"My name's Shannon Murphy and I just moved here to the house across from Sarah Bristoll's place."

"You mean Judge Benson's homestead? I didn't know that house was for sale."

"No, I'm only renting it. It's my first day here and I had to come and say hello to this handsome fellow."

Barney was sniffing her hand through the fence. She stroked the dog's muzzle.

"Well, come through the gate here to say hello proper-like."

Shannon walked in. The large dog jumped on her, knocking her down.

"Barney! Off!"

The dog jumped away. Shannon knelt before the dog, laughing and rubbing its large head.

"Barney, you're quite a big boy. I bet you eat them out of house and home."

"He's fine. But he's a lot of work. Dad and I have had him four years. He's still like a big puppy, really."

"Where did you move from?"

"We lived in Woodsdale. A ways from here in south-east Vermont. Lived in a cabin down there."

"I don't know that area. I moved from East Cabot."

"Did you know the person who owned the house you're in? You related to him?"

"No, I didn't know him. Heard about him. And his dog."

"Oh, Chauncey, yes, she's a special girl. So loved that dog!"

"You knew her? Did you come visit them up here?"

"Well, we once had her when she was quite young. It's a long story. But I knew her so well. She was a service dog for Dirck. He's now passed away, and not sure what happened to Chauncey exactly. I'd sure love to see her again, though."

A deep voice called from the house.

"Joannie? Are you out here?"

"Out here, daddy. Come out!"

A large man stepped unsteadily from the house, deliberately taking each step down. He limped across the uneven field.

"This is Shannon. She moved into Judge Benson's homestead just yesterday. Renting it."

The man's face was cleanly shaven and ruddy with deep-set dark eyes framed in wrinkles. It was an honest face yet one filled with some uncertainty. He extended his thick hand.

"Glad to make your acquaintance, Miss. Name's Jake."

She took his hand. A sudden awareness swept through her.

She stared at him.

"Have we ever met, Jake?"

He let go of her hand and looked down. His past had been uneven and suspicious. Perhaps they had crossed paths in earlier years down in Woodsdale during his troubled drinking days. Perhaps she was connected with the police or knew about his theft of the dog years earlier. He stepped back.

"No, don't believe we have," he said and turned awkwardly back to the house.

"Don't take notice of him. Dad's kind-a moody sometimes," said Joannie.

Shannon smiled uneasily as she watched Jake walk away.

"Anyways, my dad lost the cabin we were in and Dirck knew him and arranged this place for us. Dad was Dirck's friend and he wanted to live up here and that's when we got Barney. Chauncey and Barney became great friends. Then, after only a couple years, one day Dirck just wasn't there and neither was his dog. Was horrible. Broke my father up good and Barney was sad for quite some time."

"How did he know Dirck Hansen?"

"It's a long story. Hey, listen, I have to get back to my schoolwork. I'm going to the Glenriver Academy now and I'm due in class. Too-da-loo!"

"Well, please bring Barney by anytime…I'd love the company. Anytime, please."

Joannie danced back to her house, leaving the dog. Shannon looked down at Barney.

"We'll, handsome boy, I guess I have to…."

The dog stared up at her intently, not moving. She knelt and held his big head, stroking his slobbering muzzle. The dog continued his unblinking stare.

"What is it, boy? What do you want?"

The dog cocked his head and let out a low guttural *ruff* and stepped back with a look of something like sorrow on his face. An image passed across Shannon's vision, the image of Barney and another dog running towards her from the distant field.

"Who are you with, Barney?"

The dog stepped forward and let out a chesty *woof.*

"Ok, handsome fellow, I'll come again and be sure I have a good treat for you next time."

She walked back to the Judge Benson's homestead. In the middle of the field, she stopped and looked about.

The yard, the meadow, the patterns of trees, the houses, all felt intimate and close somehow. She knew there must be a purpose to her being here, something she must do.

She walked home, her heart beating like the wings of the sparrows that swirled above her.

15

The first night in the homestead, Shannon lay in a sleepless dream. The rustling of the trees brought forth a continuous surf, slamming doors and rattling windows throughout the large house. A nighttime habit, she bunched the bedspread and pillows along her side, hugging the length of the stretched-out pile through the night. In half sleep, she smoothed the fine tufts of the bedspread as she traced the contours of an imagined dog's muzzle, down the curve of its shoulders and back up to the head with its fine filamentary whiskers arched over fictional eyes.

The wind blew across her, and amidst the soothing sound, she could hear a low and soft moan, not a sad sound, but one more of contentment. The sound continued through the night as she floated through the dream. She drew in a deep breath and hugged the bedspread along its length.

"I'm here. Right here," she whispered into the silence.

By morning, the winds had stopped and it was peaceful. She drew out of bed for the day, now her second in the homestead.

A story deadline was near—it was Tuesday and Bud had asked Shannon to send the next installment by Wednesday but she hadn't really formed much of it yet. The first installment had turned out fine after some edits. Calls were coming into the *Caledonian Record* for more. She finished her breakfast and went to the office in the downstairs bedroom. Everything was long-hand until ready for transcription with the typewriter. This installment would cover Pownal and North Pownal, then Groton. And Glenriver. All with traces of a similar history and stories. She looked at what she started so far:

In the storied history of Vermont, one remarkable story stands clear of the others. For it had been told by the local magistrate in Glenriver about a mysterious dog that had roamed the town at night, never appearing in the day, and on the night Grover's Corner Feedstore had caught fire, it was said that old man Grover had gotten trapped in the blaze but that the dog had run after him, dragging him to safety. The man lived but never saw the dog after that night. Local gossip claimed the dog belonged to an old woodcarver that lived in the village of Glenriver, but nobody could confirm it, and years later, it showed up outside the house of Lucy Matters and her sister Grace, who wrote in their diary about a ghost dog that would come in the night and sit in the field across from their house. Then, in the early 1900s, stories about the dog again surfaced and people claimed to have seen it and, while early photographers tried to capture it, the dog remained elusive, existing only in the sorted stories told at town meetings and sewing circles and through rum-soaked tales at local taverns.

Then, in recent history, there was some speculation that the dog had come back but this time as a service dog named who belonged to the retired Army Captain Dirck Hansen who lived in Judge Benson's homestead.

A chesty bark rang out.

Barney was at the kitchen door. She opened it and the dog waddled in, pushing up against her, knocking her to the ground. She hugged his neck.

"Barney boy, why have you come here? Did you get loose?"

The big dog stared at her. His brown eyes were nearly hidden within the black fur that surrounded them, yet she could see in them great affection.

"You're a handsome dog, Barney. Why don't you come in here and sit with me?"

She walked to the living room and plopped down on the leather couch and raised her hand. Barney leapt up and pushed into her, pinning her against the armrest. The dog nuzzled in against her and licked her face. She lay wedged between the couch arm and dog and closed her eyes. The dog fell asleep against her, snoring loudly. Ten minutes past.

"Barney! Where are you?"

The dog leapt to the ground and lumbered to the kitchen door.

It was Joannie.

"Oh Barney! Here's where you were—had me so worried!"

"She just showed up at my door…don't know how she got out," said Shannon.

"Oh, he's clever. He watches me move the latch on the gate and now knows how to work it," Joannie laughed.

"Well, it was a pleasure having him here. He's such an affectionate boy. He just jumped up on the couch and pressed against me. Almost like he was protecting me."

"Really? I've never seen Barney do that. He's never come up on the couch with me like that."

"Seemed like he needed to assure that I was okay."

Barney was sitting beside Shannon, staring up at her. She smiled at the dog.

"I once saw him protect my father when he had fainted and fallen in our house. Barney was right there, nudging his face and arms trying to get him to wake up."

"That sounds like something a service dog would do."

"Well, Barney came from an outfit in upstate New York called Canine Assisting Soldiers. They train service and therapy dogs. Barney was going to be trained as a therapy boy but he didn't pass. Just too goofy and distracted, I guess. That's the same outfit where

Chauncey was trained for Dirck Hansen. You should have met her. She's such a beautiful Golden Retriever and just amazingly sweet and protective."

Shannon stared at Barney. The dog was fixed on her.

"Do you know where Chauncey went? Is she still living?"

"Oh, God, I wish I knew. I'd give anything to see that sweet girl again. I think she must be about seven or maybe eight years old by now. We of course knew her when she was a lot younger. I loved that dog so much!"

"That was before you lived here? How did you know her?"

"It's kinda a sad story, but when I was a lot younger, around eleven or so, I had lost my own dog, Mac. He was a young cocker spaniel I loved so but he got run over by a truck where we used to live in Woodsdale. I thought I would die back then."

"Oh Joannie, I can't even imagine how horrible that would have been."

"Yeah, well, my dad couldn't stand to see me so depressed so he got me another dog: Chauncey. He had taken her one day in a park near our place and he didn't tell me she was someone else's dog. I named her *Kady*. I loved that dog so much. But poor girl was so unhappy about being away from her own home."

"Your father *stole* her?" Shannon stared at the girl in disbelief.

"Well, yeah, he did. I didn't know anything about it until a long time later. That was after Chauncey ran off. She just took off into the woods one day and never came back!"

"What happened to her?"

"It was a big story. Took her almost two years before she finally found Dirck. Chauncey saved his life in this very house. Some of the story wasn't reported because Dirck never told them the whole story afterward."

"And you don't know where she lives now?"

"No. I didn't even know Dirck died but we later found out and dad and we went to his funeral back in late November. Chauncey was there but I didn't get to pet her…she was too sad. That's the last time I saw her and after that, the house was empty."

"How did he die?"

"Don't know but I think he was sick. He had taken a lot of drugs for his PTSD and stuff."

"PTSD? Oh, Chauncey was a PTSD service dog?"

"Yeah, dad told me that. After all that happened, he and Dirck became close friends and dad wanted to move closer to Dirck for visits. They are both veterans. After Dirck died, we decided to stay here anyways."

"I asked the person who rented me the house about the dog but she didn't talk to me about it for some reason."

"Why is Chauncey so important to you? I mean why do you want to know so much about her?"

Shannon stared down at Barney, who was lying on her feet. Her brow furled.

"It's difficult to say really. I saw a picture of her in a small photo that was left behind. She was such a beautiful dog. I just feel like I know her."

"Yeah. Oh, wait…I have some pictures."

Joannie pulled out her smartphone and started swiping through hundreds of small bright images. Like most teenagers, her whole life was on the phone.

"Here's some. These were taken about a year before Dirck passed away."

Shannon leaned against the girl as she swiped through the bright images. She pointed at one.

"Wait, let me see that one."

Joannie handed her the phone. On the screen was a closeup of Chauncey looking up at Joannie. The dog's eyes and brow formed triangles, giving her a look of concern, almost of sorrow. Her ears were perched forward as if listening to someone. The image was powerful.

"Yeah, I remember that day. Dirck had gone through a bad week. My dad said he had gotten sick and stuff and had to go to the hospital. Chauncey was by his side every second, but she was worried, I could tell. I knew when that dog was happy, and when she wasn't. She wasn't in that picture."

She couldn't take her eyes off the dog's face.

"Oh, God…I hope she's okay now."

The screen lit up Shannon's face. She looked lost.

"Joannie, I have to meet her. I mean, I really want to see Chauncey. I wonder if…."

Joannie took back her phone.

"Well, like I said, I don't know where she went. I don't even know who owns this house now," she said as she hooked Barney's leash. "I have to go. I'll make sure Barney's gate is locked better."

Joannie rushed out the back door towards home, the dog lumbering next to her.

Shannon watched them from the kitchen window.

She must have upset the girl. After all, why would she ask so many questions about Chauncey? She was finding it difficult to justify her feelings or even understand them. But she couldn't stop thinking about the dog and what had become of her. What were those voices calling to her? What was it she was supposed to do?

She had no answers and worrying about the dog's whereabouts would be the least of what she would face here at Judge Benson's homestead.

16

Dru's cellphone buzzed. She was on her way back with Callie from the Chittenden Nursing Home. It was mid-day and she had hoped to make it back to CAS by five from the southern Vermont location.

Callie had been specifically requested by Mrs. Turnbill, a frail ninety-two-year-old woman who had been given only three months to live. Of the dogs that the woman had met, Callie was the only one who made a difference in her mood and today, the visit had been nearly two hours long, enough for the frail woman to finally relax and sleep.

"Hello?"

"Hi, Dru, this is Shannon. Sorry to bother you but the furnace went out and I have no heat or hot water. I tried the Glenriver number you gave me, but John Higgins is on vacation. It's been out for a couple days now and thought you could help."

"I know a local guy, Dana, who can help, I think. Let me call and I can swing up there in an hour since I'm in your vicinity."

"Thank you."

When Dru pulled into the driveway an hour later, a black truck was in the driveway. The tech was in the basement. She left Callie in the car and walked to the side door.

"Hi Shannon. See a truck out there. I guess Dana's here."

"Yes, he's in the basement pulling the furnace apart. I very much appreciate it. Difficult without heat at night. Starting to get cold now that fall's about here."

"Well, I thought I'd stop around to make sure it gets fixed and see if there's anything else I can help with. It's been a while since I was here."

Shannon heard a bark. It came from Dru's car. A large black dog was shifting about and barking through the cracked window.

"That's Callie. She's a therapy dog I am working with at the Chittenden Home. We were on our way home. Not sure why she's acting up like that. She's normally pretty quiet."

The dog began crying at the cracked window. Shannon smiled.

"Oh, please let her out!"

"I don't want to bother you. She's fine in the car."

"I would most like to meet her. May I?"

Dru went out and opened the car door. Callie bounded out in a wide circle and came at Shannon, but stopped before her and sat, her large tongue lolling about.

"Oh, she's so well behaved!"

"Yes, she's been trained. She's a certified therapy dog. A great one, too. Has been for a couple of years."

Callie stared up at Shannon and cocked her head as if waiting for something. A signal of some sort. She knelt to the dog and lightly caressed her muzzle. Callie leaned forward and nuzzled her head into her shoulders. They remained still.

Dru stared at them in disbelief.

"She seems so drawn to you. That's unusual for her. She's normally cautious with strangers."

Shannon didn't hear her. She leaned into the dog's strong neck and breathed in. The dog felt familiar. Smelled familiar. Her heart raced.

Dru shook her head. As a trainer and knowing Callie well, the dog's reaction puzzled her. And worried her. She had remembered the woman questioning her about Chauncey, where she had gone, what had become of her. And now this. It wasn't a threat but it was still odd. She had never seen Callie take to anyone like this.

"Dru, can I just take her out into the field and play for a bit? I think she'd like that."

Callie looked up at Shannon. Her bright eyes were steady. She nodded to the dog.

"Yes, girl. I understand," Shannon said.

And with that, she stood, and without a word from Dru, walked into the field. Callie's head was fixed towards Shannon as she trotted in step with her. They looked like a well-trained team, handler and dog walking through a field trial. Shannon raised her arm and pointed to the field. Callie raced towards the far stand of firs in the distance, galloping at an impressive pace. She clapped once and the dog froze and snapped her head back. She clapped twice and Callie turned sharply and ran back, stopping abruptly in her tracks before her. The two walked back together in silence.

Dru had never seen Callie that obedient.

A voice from the house broke the silence.

"All done," said Dana. The technician's blue overalls were covered in soot. "Just a clogged ignitor. Cleaned her on up. Runs good now."

She went to pay the man and didn't look back at Callie who was sprawled across Shannon's legs.

"I'm not sure what to say. Callie seems to somehow know you, She's only obedient around her trainers. And never like that, really. Have you ever worked with dogs before?"

Shannon stroked the dog's sleek black coat.

"I can't explain it, Dru. I never have worked with dogs but I just feel at home with her. I wish she could stay here. I know she can't but I feel at home with her."

"No, she can't. We have to continue her training if she's going to keep her certification for a therapy dog, and she's in high demand. If I have a chance, I'll try to bring her around again, but we're over in Baker's Mills, so it's a bit of a trip."

"Baker's Mills? In New York? Isn't that near Siamese Pond Wilderness? I've been there! At the Round Top Barn Inn just outside Johnsberg Ferry, near Baker's Mills. It's beautiful!"

"When did you say you were there?"

"It was just after Valentine's day this year. My sister and I vacationed there."

The dates lined up. It was late last February when Chauncey got loose and ran up to the Round Top Barn.

Dru frowned. Callie's reaction to Shannon and this new revelation began to seriously concern her but she couldn't quite put any of it together.

"Well, we have to get back home. Your furnace is working now and you should have hot water. If anything else causes problems, let me know."

She knelt and held out her hand but Callie didn't move.

"Come on girl. Time to go."

The dog continued to sit by Shannon. She gave her a nod. Callie rose to Dru.

As they drove away, Callie's face was pressed against the closed window, watching the woman as she disappeared.

The drive back to CAS was enveloped in mystery. Dru couldn't shake the image of Callie with Shannon, how the dog had bonded to her, how perfectly she handled her dog. She arrived at nightfall and the lights in the facility were still on. She led Callie into her room and sat with her, stroking her head, watching her for any reaction that might give her answers. But Callie looked up at her in the same way—obedient, ready for training. But it wasn't the same look she had given Shannon.

That had been different.

"What is it, girl? What did you see there?"

Dave Ballard walked past the door.

"How was Callie's training today?"

"She was a star, as always. Got Mrs. Turnbill in a good frame of mind. Allowed the poor woman to finally settle down and sleep. It was a good visit…but something happened."

Dave walked in.

"What? Is Callie okay?"

"She's fine but I took her over to the Judge Benson homestead. The new renter had a furnace broken and I let Callie out to play. I can't explain it but Callie and the woman, Shannon, took to each other in the most unusual way. They instantly bonded and it was as if Callie recognized her and wanted to soothe the woman for some reason. She buried her head in her embrace and it looked like Callie taking care of one of our patients. That, and the dog was super obedient with her, responding to her commands, just like in a field trial. It was almost frightening."

"That's unusual. Perhaps she smelled something on the woman that drew her."

"Yes, I thought that too. But this was combined with something else. Remember in late February when Chauncey ran up the hill to that inn?"

"Yes, that *was* odd."

"Turns out that my renter, Shannon, was up there vacationing at the Round Top Barn Inn. In late February, at the same time we found Chauncey up there. I think Shannon had just left the Inn when she was up there."

Dave Ballard's eyes widened. He leaned forward.

"What? The woman had just been there? My God, Chauncey must have smelled her and was after her for some reason!"

"This really worries me, Dave. I don't know much about this woman, Shannon Murphy. Only that she's from East Cabot and works as a writer for the *Caledonian Record* there. Good references. Nothing seemed of the ordinary about her. Maybe I need to find out more."

"Well, it's curious. But I wouldn't worry too much about it. It's not as if there had been a bad reaction from Callie. I guess I wouldn't take her back there if you have to return."

"Probably not. I'm so tired from the day, and this just threw me. I'll take her back to the pen."

Chauncey was curled in her bed when Callie was led in. Her head snapped up.

"Here's your friend," Dru said and opened the enclosure.

Chauncey stood and walked slowly to her companion, her ears flat, her tail down. She walked around Callie, sniffing her intently.

Dru could tell something was off.

Chauncey's nose explored Callie's neck, her face and ears. She began to whine and her furry tail began to swing.

"What is it, girl? What do you smell? What…?"

Callie lay before her companion in submission. Chauncey stepped around Callie, her nose to her body as she took in the dog. Callie remained still, somehow knowing that her companion was recognizing Shannon's sent on her. Dru watched from the corner of the pen. The smelling continued for nearly an hour.

At some point, Chauncey sat back and looked up at Dru, her eyes again forming those triangles, lamblike, that look of concern, something she had seen in the hospitals when she knew there was a loss.

She whined again. Dru knelt to her.

"Oh, girl, what is it? What has you so worried?"

Dru stroked her back, her sad head. Chauncey placed her chin on her companion's neck and closed her eyes. After she was sure Chauncey was comfortable, Dru backed away. As she walked out of the pen, she took one look back. The night light cast a dim light in the pen. Dru could see Chauncey's eyes were open, staring out the far window in sorrow.

The whistling from the floor registers woke Shannon. It was cold and the furnace had just kicked on. The clock on the mantle read 6:30 p.m. but she wasn't sure how long she had been laying on the couch. She felt heavy, her usual energy drained and she struggled to get upstairs. The early autumn weather had brought a steady rain that seemed peaceful but it began to rapidly pick up.

She looked out the picture window to the field beyond. It was dark, darker than it should have been for an early evening this time of year. From across the field, thick grey and black clouds hung oppressively low in the sky, oozing and billowing as they as they advanced towards the house. Lightning flashed in blinding streaks icily illuminating the trees as they cast their long ghostly shadows under the charcoaled sky.

A sudden pressure erupted against her, an explosion, as if the sky had been gripped at its corners and was violently shaken out and down upon her. The room exploded in light.

Her heart raced. She fell to her knees and crawled to the edge of the bed. Sheets of water pulsed at the windows and roared against the metal roof as if an army approached. She looked out.

Between blinding flashes, she could just make out the flickering images of bodies strewn along the field's length, lifeless figures scattered about, and amidst the pulsing thunder, she heard guns firing, munitions exploding, yelling and screaming of men.

The tremendous clangor of battle, the furnace roar of explosions surrounded her as she lay clenched in a ball.

"Oh God! What is happening? Please stop!"

She pressed pillows to her head and squeezed her eyes shut.

In the darkness before her, a bloody and grim figure of a man appeared, his eyes vacant, his arms out.

The soldier's heart is a broken heart…I carry the memories of pain, of loss, of death in battle.

She leapt up, running through the dark room, slamming into walls and furniture. She scrambled up the stairs and dove into the bathroom, turned on the shower, and jumped under the cold water to shock it away.

She wept in the darkness, her heart pounding uncontrollably.

From Shannon's crumpled body, mortal fear spewed up and out through the open bathroom window.

The acrid smell of fear, of foul cooking meat, spread across the fields and forests, rapidly widening throughout the land like a thick bank of fetid smoke.

17

Chauncey lay quietly, listening for the sound of Dru's footsteps. She hadn't moved all night, still wrapped tightly around Callie. She knew today was therapy day but she didn't want to move.

Throughout the long night, she again had dreamed of Dirck. She could see him, hear him clearly. *Chauncey, come to me*, his soothing deep voice calling to her, his strong, certain hands caressing her back. She breathed in deeply, trying to retain the scent fixed within her nose. The essence of it surrounded Callie, and it both comforted and made her heart race. Helping the sick and dying raised her spirits and had made her feel useful again, but she still hadn't shaken her heartache from Dirck's loss, and this new strong scent again brought forth buried sadness. It was as if she had been transported back to that day nearly a year ago when Dirck had left her.

She took in another deep breath and closed her heavy eyes.

The far gate clanged. Dru appeared at the pen door.

It was 5 a.m.

"Hello beautiful girls. I hope you slept well. Today's a working day for you both."

Chauncey didn't move. Callie was still trying to wake from a deep sleep. She opened the gate.

"Okay, girls, let's get moving. Callie, come on girl."

Callie jumped up but as Dru donned her halter, Chauncey stood and protested in a sharp bark.

"What's this? Don't worry, you're going too girl," she said and attached her vest.

Today, Callie would travel to Glensfalls Hospice to visit a new patient with terminal cancer and had only weeks to live. Chauncey would ride with them would be taken further east to the Veteran's Hospital in Goshen, Vermont. Her new assignment was to visit a depressed soldier with PTSD who had lost his legs years ago in Iraq and was awaiting his own CAS service dog.

The hospital had been one that Dirck had visited years before he was paired with Chauncey.

After breakfast, they left. Callie leapt into the van, followed by Chauncey, who snuggled in close to her. Dru and her trainer, Maggie Kendrick, drove off to Glensfalls, the first stop on the two-hour ride.

After dropping off Callie and Maggie, Dru drove Chauncey another hour east to Goshen. It was a small town originally called "Chepontuc," a Mohawk word meaning "hard to get around" because of its confusing landscape and odd small roads leading nowhere. The VA sat within miles of these untraveled country roads and unmapped trails, deep within the woods.

Goshen sat just over the New York border in Vermont, eighty miles west of her former home in Glenriver.

They arrived mid-morning. It was a sunny but cool autumn day, perfect for dog and man to be outside. Dru hoped the veteran would be willing to work with Chauncey in the facility courtyard. Today would just be just getting acquainted, man to dog.

As she walked Chauncey towards the building, she thought about Dirck and how Chauncey had transformed the broken veteran. She hoped this new fellow would take to her as much as Dirck had.

They were met by Grace, a nurse, and Rusty, a veteran who worked at the VA. They knelt to greet Chauncey who normally would be wiggling with excitement with new people. But she was distracted.

"Say hello, Chauncey," said Dru.

The dog stared blankly beyond them.

"Chauncey girl, come on."

Dru thought she might be confused by the new surroundings and led her around the back courtyard. After ten minutes, she returned to Grace and Rusty.

"Say hello."

Chauncey wagged her tail. They reached out to her but she remained oddly detached. It reminded Dru of her dog's early training when she had returned from the Pups For Prisoners program, a time when she distrusted everyone after losing her handler in her early life. It had taken months for her to come back, and when she had first met Dirck, also a lost soul, the two had found salvation in one another.

She was puzzled by Chauncey's withdrawal. Just a month ago, she was bright and brilliant, eager to meet new people, wanting to help her patients in hospitals.

Not today, it appeared.

"We'll bring Brig out. Brig Taylor. He's received prosthetic legs but refuses to put them on and is still in his wheelchair. He's depressed and angry, so go easy with him," Rusty said.

The door opened and Rusty wheeled out Brig. The vet wore dark wraparound mirrored sunglasses and was slumped in his wheelchair, staring down. His prosthetic legs sat in the chair next to him. His long stringy hair and unkempt grey beard gave him a lost, almost angry look. He didn't make eye contact. He clearly didn't want to be here.

"Brig, we'd like you to meet Dru Vaughn. She's the owner of Canine Assisting Soldiers in New York, the place where your new service dog will come from. She's brought Chauncey, a therapy dog. She had been a service dog for Dirck Hansen, another veteran," Grace said.

Brig listened but didn't move. He looked almost paralyzed, frozen within his wheelchair prison. Dru motioned Chauncey to sit in front of him.

She looked up at Brig. The man seemed familiar to her. For a moment, there was no movement but after another minute, Brig brought his shaky hand up to his sunglasses and peeled them away to get a better look at the dog.

His eyes were stark and blank. Chauncey looked up at him. She could see in his eyes the same thing as she had seen in Dirck's when they had first met. Deeply wounded and lost.

Brig could see the dog connected with him.

"Hello Chauncey," he said.

His voice was deep and raspy. He smiled slightly, revealing his crooked yellowed teeth. Chauncey stood and her tail fanned slowly about to let Brig know she was with him.

Because they were in an enclosed courtyard, Dru removed her lead to give her freedom. Brig's hand reached down and Chauncey stepped forward to accept him.

"Good dog," he said and ruffled her thick fur.

She licked Brig's puffy hand. The veteran straightened up in his chair. Chauncey moved closer and sniffed Brig's pants, which were folded and pinned up around his stumps.

"Lost 'em, girl. Lost 'em in battle. Tough thing. Can't walk now. Tough, girl."

The dog understood the man's loss. He was just like Dirck. She stared into Brig's eyes with understanding.

"You know what it's like helping us broken soldiers, don't you girl? I can see that."

Nobody spoke but Brig. Rusty and Grace slowly shook their heads in amazement at how a dog could lead an angry broken man out of his misery, even just for a moment. Dru understood.

"Brig, would you like to be alone with Chauncey? She knows how to walk with the wheelchair," she said.

"Yes ma'am, we'd like that," he said and unlocked his chair.

The veteran wheeled slowly away through the lane of sycamore trees, Chauncey walking by his side, occasionally looking up to him for direction. They stopped at the far end of the long yard.

Dru and the VA team couldn't hear them.

Brig was bent over his chair gesturing this way, then that, out to the field beyond, back to his chest, animated, alive. He was smiling. Chauncey sat attentively by his side, cocking her head back and forth as she took in the man's story, letting him unload his burdens onto her, as she had for so many years with Dirck. She understood Brig's loss and the need for warmth, for trust. Chauncey was a deeply sensitive dog but also deeply wounded by her own loss. She put her paw up on Brig's arm as he talked.

"You know how we lost what we used to have, don't you girl? You understand. Your man, Dirck, he was lost just like me. We don't know where to go or what to do sometimes. We've lost our way. But you can help bring us back, back home. You need us to help guide you, too. It's tough being out here on your own. Loss seems forever sometimes, doesn't it, girl?"

Chauncey deeply felt Brig's loss. She raised up on his wheelchair to him. He held her. She sniffed him. He had that sad smell just like Dirck and she pictured him sitting in the wheelchair.

At the other side of the yard, Dru turned to Rusty.

"This is a good sign. Chauncey knows the despair these veterans feel, what they've lost. It'll help me get him a dog like Chauncey. We have another Golden Retriever named 'Tess' that would be good for him."

After nearly a half hour, Brig wheeled slowly back, Chauncey ambling by his side. They both looked like they had been together for years.

"I'm glad you had a good talk, Brig," said Rusty.

"We understand one another. You wouldn't understand. But she does," he said pointing down to her.

"We will bring her back again, Brig," Dru said to him.

"Yes, ma'am, I hope so. She understands me."

The man wheeled himself back into the side door but turned back to Chauncey.

"Be good, girl. I'll see you soon and we'll have another good talk, I promise. Just between you and me, girl."

As he left, Brig wanted Chauncey to know he was still brave against his crippling fear. She had given him that courage in just the short time they had together.

Brig struggled to the edge of his chair and fixed his prosthetic legs onto his limbs. He awkwardly stood and with a grin, sharply saluted the dog, then turned and swayed uneasily back through the door under his own proud power, leaving his wheelchair behind.

Chauncey could still smell Brig well after he disappeared from sight. The smell of sadness and fear mixed with love lingered in her. Just like Dirck.

From the opposite end of the courtyard across the stone fence, a rush of wind swept over her. It carried a remembered scent.

Unmistakably Dirck Hansen's fear!

She rose and pulled in the heavy air. It flooded her brain.

She had to find him.

She nervously looked about the yard, searching for a way out. The gate was open.

She raced through it and out towards the forest beyond.

In seconds, she was gone.

18

Barney was at Shannon's kitchen door, swiping frantically at it. The dog had again escaped and Joannie had caught up with him.

"Barney! What…why are you over here? What is it, boy?"

The dog barked at the door.

Joannie called out.

"Shannon?"

There was silence. She yelled up to the open dormer window.

"Are you there?"

She could just make out a cry from the window. The back door was open and Barney pushed through it and ran past her, leading her into the upstairs bathroom. She followed.

The woman was sprawled out in the shower under the running cold water. She was weeping.

Joannie turned off the shower and knelt to her, smoothing hair away from her face.

"Oh my God, Shannon. What happened? Did you fall? Are you okay?

Barney licked her face, bolting the woman into consciousness.

"Don't know how long I've been here…not sure how I got here."

"Why were you under the shower with your cloths on? What happened to you?"

There were no answers but Joannie knew she had to get her into dry cloths and to bed. She pulled out her phone and dialed home.

"Daddy, I'm here at Judge Benson's. Found Shannon on the floor. Call 9-1-1. Something has happened to her!"

Joannie dressed the woman in dry sweatpants and shirt and lifted her into bed.

The paramedics arrived.

"Up here!" she yelled out the window.

Melony, the lead medic and her assistant, a younger woman, ran into the bedroom. Shannon was pale and her heart raced. The medic hooked her up to monitors.

"Your blood pressure is normal," said Melony.

"I think I had a panic attack…my name's Shannon."

"I need to listen to your heart."

The paramedic lifted her sweatshirt but hesitated when she saw the long pink scar running along her breastbone.

"Did you have heart surgery recently?"

"Received a transplant nearly a year ago."

Joannie looked down at Shannon, her eyes wide. She hadn't noticed the huge scar when she had dressed her. It was shocking.

"Your heart rate is rather fast, but it sounds okay…no abnormalities. You think something panicked you?"

"Can't remember. I think it was a frightening dream. Something about war and death. There was a storm. I heard voices and saw terrible things."

Melony hooked Shannon to EKG leads and read it from her phone. The paramedic pulled out a satellite phone.

"Dr. Briggs. Melony here. We're in Glenriver to check on a woman who apparently had a panic attack. She's a transplant recipient but her vitals are normal, heart sounds and EKG look okay. Sending it through now. She's alert and talking fine. No signs of a stroke."

As the paramedic talked, Joannie helped Barney climb onto the bed. He splayed his large body out, his head at hers, licking her cheek. Shannon held his head and smiled.

"Okay, Shannon, we don't see any reason to bring you in today. EKG normal. I think you had some panic reaction from a memory or dream and you need to rest for the day. Call us if anything changes."

As the paramedics were leaving, Jake Tollinger approached.

"Is she okay?"

"She's fine…she just had a bad dream or something," said Melony as she loaded her equipment into the ambulance. "Thanks for calling it in. She's upstairs in bed with a dog and the young woman who found her."

As Jake descended the short stairwell down into the bedroom, he stopped and looked about. He had had seen this bedroom once with Dirck but he felt uneasy being here.

"Shannon's okay. But wow! She has a new heart and a big long scar!" Joannie blurted out.

Her lack of tact often seeped out of her otherwise mature demeanor.

"Well, yes, I was a recipient for a new heart that saved my life," Shannon said.

"Wow, do you know whose heart it is? Like, do they tell you who it came from and all?"

"No, I will never find that out. The donor explicitly did not want that revealed."

Jake stood away from the bed. The whole situation and being here made him unsettled. He walked around the large room, looking everywhere but the bed. He spotted an alcove on the wall.

"I seem to remember that Dirck used to have a hidden safe or opening somewhere around here," Jake said as he felt the wall.

He noticed a seam.

"Yes, there's an opening here. Dirck had kept some of his documents and maybe photos in here. He showed it to me that summer we first came up here."

"What's in there?" said Shannon.

"Don't know. Since you're now living here, maybe we should find out."

He pushed on the wall. A door tripped open. Inside was a shoebox with several photos and a small camera.

Shannon frowned.

"I don't know. Should we be looking at this stuff? Perhaps I need to tell my landlady Dru about this."

Joannie looked down at her.

"Dru? Do you mean the woman who owns the dog training place, Dirck's friend?" said Joannie.

"I only know she owns this house now. She's the one that rented it to me. She's over in New York, somewhere at a Baker's Mills address. At least, that's where I send my rent checks."

Jake looked at his daughter.

"Dru Vaughn has a dog training place there. Think it's called Canines Assisting Soldiers. It's where Barney came from. She's the one who trained Chauncey for Dirck years ago. She had brought her to Dirck's funeral."

"If that's the same woman, she must have taken Chauncey out to her training kennel up there. I imagine that's what happened to her," Shannon said.

Yes, Chauncy's probably with Dru—I know she wouldn't have let Chauncey go to another soldier," Jake said.

He put placed the photographs on the bed. They were grouped with rubber bands. There were old black and white photos of soldiers, men in their uniforms standing at attention for the camera. Smaller color photographs showed Dirck Hansen in his younger years with a woman, some with an older man. Perhaps his wife or sister and father.

"Dirck was certainly a handsome man," Shannon said as she sorted through them.

The photos seemed to be arranged chronologically. She picked up another stack. Pictures of the Judge Benson homestead, some during summer with the wide green field, some in the winter with snow blanketing the grounds and house.

She reached a grouping of photographs with Chauncey. When he had first brought his new service dog home, Dirck had photographed her almost every day. That was when had been just three.

Shannon leaned over the color images. They showed the dog in profile, lying on the porch, standing at attention, some looking at the photographer, Dirck. She was magnificent. Her feathery gold coat and balanced body beamed confidence and purpose. She looked cheerful, enthusiastic, full of life, eager to please, to work. One picture was a closeup of Chauncey staring up at the camera. She had a short snout and small pendant ears, giving her an eternal puppy look. Her eyes were an unusual amber color and her expression seemed thoughtful, almost human.

She brought her hand to her mouth.

"What's wrong? Are you okay? Another bad memory?" Joannie said.

"I'm okay," she said through her hand. "I just felt light headed. My God, I'm sure Chauncey is with my landlord! Dru was just out here recently and had brought another dog with her, a black Labrador Retriever, a beautiful girl."

"Oh wow! That's Callie. We know her too!" said Joannie.

Shannon's eyes widened.

"The two dogs are really close. They were on the run together years ago. We think Chauncey saved Callie's life more than once," said Joannie.

"That dog, Callie, took strongly to me for some reason. She was so obedient. It was as if I knew her and had trained her. It upset Dru."

"Dirck helped train Callie after Chauncey had returned home. She really took to Dirck," Jake said.

Shannon picked up the last stack of photographs. They showed pictures of Dru and Callie with Chauncey, taken by Dirck's veteran friends.

"I can't believe I'm seeing these photographs. It's wonderful."

Jake looked over her shoulder.

"I am a veteran, like Dirck. I had originally taken Chauncey as a young dog. That would have been just after she had been brought here, just about like…right here," he said and pointed to an early photo of Chauncey in front of the homestead.

Joannie looked at her father, shaking her head.

"She doesn't want to hear about this, daddy."

"Yes, I do. Go on. Please go on," Shannon said.

"I stole the young dog for Joannie here. She had been so heartbroken at the loss of her pup. That was so long ago. I lost my way back then. All I had wanted was to bring back my daughter's happiness," he said and put his arm around Joannie.

"How long was she gone?"

"She ran away from us just a few months after we brought her home. It took nearly two years before she found her way back to Dirck. He had almost died at the hands of men who had taken

Chauncey after I did, men who had robbed him and almost killed him. The dogs saved him and Dru. Here in this very house!"

Shannon stared at him, shaking her head.

"Yes, I read some of that in the *Glenriver Journal* down at the historic society. But I didn't know the whole story. My God, their reunion must have been incredible!"

"Oh, yes. That dog and Dirck were inseparable. I've never seen such love between a dog and her master."

"When Dirck died, it must have killed her!" Shannon said. Tears were dripping onto her sweatshirt.

"One day, he was gone and the townfolk didn't say much. We went to his funeral here in Glenriver. Chauncey was there with Dru and some fellow," Jake said.

Shannon stared down at the photographs. Some of them were of Chauncey and Dru before she had met Dirck, when she was trained at CAS in New York. She remembered being in Siamese Ponds last February, the images and sounds she had heard. That must have been right near Baker's Mills and CAS. She tried to piece the mystery together. She kept sorting through the images.

At the bottom of the stacks was a manila envelope. Inside was an large color photograph of Dirck and Chauncey that had been taken by Dave Ballard the day Dirck left CAS with his new service dog. Dirck was dressed in his green Captain's uniform, standing proudly at attention with a wide grin, his dog sitting by his side, her head slightly cocked up towards Dirck. It was the photograph that had been seen by millions of people throughout the world when Chauncey had disappeared.

It was the same image of the man she had seen that night outside this house. She shuddered.

Jake looked away. That was the photograph on the poster he discovered after he had stolen Chauncey and realized the dog had belonged to a fellow soldier.

"I couldn't…still can't…forgive myself for stealing that dog," Jake said as he stared out the window.

"Daddy, don't keep beating yourself up about that. You did it for me, and I love you for that. It's okay now."

The three sat on the bed amidst the photographs, wading through an afternoon of grief, revelation, and love. Shannon felt warm and close. She was elated to see the pictures and knowing more of the story.

"I can't explain it to you but these photos just draw me in so strongly. Chauncey, Dirck, Dru. Even Callie. I can't understand it. It's so different than my experience growing up. I never felt close to anyone or anything, not even the puppy I once had. I couldn't bond with the dog."

"Maybe living here brought all that out. Something about being here maybe changed you," Joannie said.

"It's almost as if I feel like Chauncey…is a part of me! I know that sounds crazy but it's how I feel."

"Maybe she is somehow," said Joannie.

"We need to let you rest now," Jake said. "If you need anything, just come by or call us."

"And I'll check on you tomorrow," said Joannie.

Barney had fallen asleep on the bed and was snoring.

"Com'on Barney boy…let's go!"

They left and Shannon lay on the bed, going back through the photographs until night fell. Her fear had vanished.

Chauncey was close, close to her heart.

19

Dru had barely seen Chauncey disappear from courtyard into the forest. It had taken seconds.

"Chauncey! Come back!" she screamed as she ran to the edge of the forest.

She called again. No response.

She knew something powerful had drawn her. Her behavior had been erratic. Running away from CAS to that Inn last February, the incident at the MRI facility, her odd behavior with Callie just days ago. It was all so uncharacteristic of the dog she loved and thought she knew so well. She couldn't imagine what was pulling her dog away from her.

She punched in Maggie Kendrick's number.

"Hi Dru, we're just finishing up, will be done…."

"Maggie, Chauncey's run off…gone! I'll have someone come pick you up. You need you to get here right away with Callie. We must find her!"

"Run off? Where?"

"Never mind, just wait for my van to pick you up. I'm mobilizing the VA folks here to get a search party out. Get ahold of Dave. We need to get pictures of Chauncey up in Goshen and surrounding towns. There's a lot of wilderness out here. She's been gone only a few minutes but could be anywhere by now."

Dru ended the call. As she stared into the woods, terrible memories flooded back. The two years she had helped Dirck look for Chauncey, those two long agonizing years of close calls and dead ends, the sightings, the tracking dog, the fear she had died. She fell to her knees and began to cry.

Chauncey's hyperosmia had overwhelmed her brain with the smell of Dirck's fear. She knew he was gone, yet the scent was distinct and real.

She ran east in a straight line through the dense forest, snapping branches, jumping rocks, not caring for her immediate surrounds. All that morning and into the afternoon, she raced flat out through into the wilderness.

By that afternoon, she reached a wide field and stopped. She took in the air but the original smell had abated. She turned this way and that, trying to orient herself to the scent that had permeated her brain for the past many hours. But now, its direction was uncertain.

And she was tired and intensely hungry. She sat at the edge of the forest staring across the expanse. She had traveled through the Vermont woods before and knew how to survive. She felt confident she could make her way and find food, but it would soon be dark and she knew the night dangers. Coyotes, wolves, hidden gorges. The autumn equinox had descended. The nights were colder now and the wildlife, both friend and foe, would be out hunting before winter. She walked to a stream and deeply quenched her thirst.

Then she caught a faint scent. The direction of it seemed to be in front of her, across the large field. She stepped forward towards an uncertain destination.

By four that afternoon, nearly two dozen men and women, even some children from the VA and the town had descended into the woods with flashlights calling for Chauncey, searching for clues. Dru had shown them pictures of her dog. The search party spent the night spread out within a twenty-mile radius. Dave Ballard and two trainers from CAS went to the small town of Goshen with posters and handouts. Some had photos of Chauncey. By that evening, posters hung from church doors, inside general stores and post offices, on trees along town common, everywhere in communities fifty miles surrounding Goshen.

As the sun rose the next morning, the search party had grown to over eighty people. Early on, some had found tufts of blonde hair and broken branches but as the search broadened, further clues eluded them. By three that afternoon, the search party was called off and the Vermont State Police was called in. Troopers remembered Chauncey from stories and accounts years ago when she had disappeared. They used a professional search tactic with demographic maps, search coordinates, even dispatching their one helicopter with infrared tracking. They brought in search dogs. The police and over one-hundred volunteers, several of them veterans, were scattered fifty miles in every direction from Goshen. News quickly spread throughout Vermont, alerting townspeople about the valuable therapy dog.

Dru and Dave stayed at the only Goshen motel to coordinate the search.

"Dave, her home in Glenriver is only about eighty miles north of here. Maybe she's headed there. Something may be pulling her up there. Not sure what, but it's possible."

"Yeah, I think that's likely. Let's get up there and see if we can find some volunteers. I'll bring posters."

Darkness had descended early in the forest and Chauncey wasn't able to make out details to navigate further. She found a dead tree stump and dug a rut for her bed. She covered herself with leaves and rugs of moss. She was invisible from sight. But not smell. She could hear the far-off howls of coyotes and wolves. She knew her scent had alerted them.

She lay awake throughout the night listening to the subtle sounds around her. She tried to find some peace in her covered bed, but Dirck was all she could think about. She had smelled his fear again. It was close, somewhere within reach. It might take just a day, maybe two.

But now she was deeply tired and closed her troubled eyes.

Throughout the long and nervous night, she lay half-awake at the unsettling rustling about her, the faint, disquieting sounds of night hunters slipping in and out through the silent shadows about her.

It was an unforgiving place for a lone dog.

20

The town of Glenriver was just waking up when Dru and Dave arrived. Mabel was unlocking the registers at Winger's Market when she heard a knock on her glass door.

"Good morning. You may remember me from a few years ago. My name is Dru Vaughn. Our dog is missing and we hope you can let us hang this poster—she's a valuable therapy dog—escaped in Goshen two days ago."

Mabel examined the poster. It had two color photos of Chauncey, a closeup of her head and another with Dru. It read:

LOST! FEMALE GOLDEN RETRIEVER EIGHT YEARS OLD. ANSWERS TO "CHAUNCEY." THIS IS A VALUABLE THERAPY DOG BELONGING TO CANINES ASSISTING SOLDIERS. $10,000 REWARD FOR HER RETURN. CONTACT DRU VAUGHN AT 518-624-3393 BAKER'S MILLS, NEW YORK.

"Is tha' same dog that was lost some years ago? Belonged to Dirck Hansen, I believe. Turned out Jake Tollinger had her at one point. Been stolen again?"

"No…she ran off at the VA down in Goshen. But yes, the same dog. We think she might be headed this way again. Possibly to the Judge Benson place up the hill. Dirck passed about a year ago and the dog has been with us. I own her now."

"Oh, heard about Dirck, yes. Terrible thing, such a nice fella. Too bad about tha' dog. Bein' lost like that is a danga'. Rememba' about her before, hope she's not…hope she's alright."

"Yes, she went through some tough things back then. We thought she was gone forever. May be headed up to her old home."

"Damned shame. There's some woman livin' up at the old homestead now, I think."

"Yes, Shannon Murphy is renting the place now."

"Yep, think she was in here not long ago. Middle aged woman, nice smile, red hair. She was in here buyin' some dog stuff. Bones, toys, treats and the like. Didn't know she had a dog."

Dru looked at Dave.

"Yes, that's the woman. But she doesn't have a dog, at least she didn't when I rented the place to her a while ago. I own that house now."

"She seemed pretty picky about them right toys, treats and all. Maybe it was for the neighbor's dog up theyah. Lots around."

"Please put my poster up and call me if you find out anything or see the dog around here."

By eleven that morning, posters were hung at Watsford's Automotive, the Glenriver Bank, the Minimart, and Isabell's Diner. Most in town knew Chauncey and word spread quickly.

Dru and Dave drove two miles up Route 5 to Judge Benson's place. It was noon but nobody was home and there was no car in the driveway. They walked through the backyard and into the woods, calling for Chauncey but by early afternoon and no signs, Dru left Shannon a note to call her. They drove to the library to hang a poster before heading back to their temporary headquarters in Goshen.

As she pulled out onto the road towards the library, Shannon drove past them. She saw Dru's camper but it didn't register.

When Shannon reached the back door, her hands were full of folders and she wedged the screen door open with her shoulder. She didn't see the folded note that had dropped to her feet.

She was anxious to get back to writing and had copied town records of Glenriver and surrounding towns. She nearly missed the cellphone buzzing in her pocket.

"Yes?" She said, out of breath.

"Hello, Shannon. This is Bud from the *Record*. Hope I'm not disturbing you."

"Just walked in, Bud. Great to hear from you. Was going to call you today. Just got some new material for some interesting stories. Realize it's been awhile and I haven't been in touch."

"Well, that's the reason I called. We haven't seen any work from you in the past month and a half. Reviewed the last story you sent in August and was baffled by it. The writing was off. And the story was mostly about some ghost dog up in that area. Not much history of the town and its people. My editors had to replace it with another story, and as you know, we're stretched thin."

"I was hoping the story would be a different angle of the town's history. Some pretty unusual aspects to it, I thought."

"John and Michaela both looked at it. It just didn't hold together. Had to trash it."

She sat down.

"Bud, I just started research on a new story for Glenriver. It's about a soldier and his dog who lived up here and their history."

"Shannon, remember how we originally framed these assignments? Our readers had asked for stories of the people, the forgotten towns, a personal love story of the left-behind and vanishing places, stories never before told, only the way you write them. At least that's what we originally talked about."

"I remember, Bud. I just have this other bent on things now that I am living here. Especially about this soldier and his dog...."

"Shannon, we don't want dog stories. The essays and editorials our readers want are about the left-behind people," Bud repeated.

"I thought that's what I was giving you, Bud."

"They aren't. That, and I'm not sure you're aware of this, but the last piece was full of spelling errors and grammar mistakes. Michaela had to spend hours rewriting it and, in the end, we knew it wouldn't work and we threw it out. It's unlike you. Are you sure you've recovered from your surgery?"

"Yes, I'm fine, Bud. You have to give me some time."

"We'll I think you need to take some time off, Shannon. I took in a temporary writer to fill in right now. Our readers are calling and writing and they're not happy."

"Time off? Are you firing me, Bud?"

"Well, I think you need some time off to get better and...."

"I'm fine. I don't need time off! I was going to start with a new piece today, right now, in fact."

"I'm sorry. I must respond to my readership. And unfortunately, I can't keep you on the payroll."

"You can't pay me either? Can we talk about this? I can come down tomorrow."

"We're talking now. I think it's best for you to take time away. We'll see how things go with my new writer. Perhaps next spring, we can revisit this."

"Spring? That's months away! Please, can we reconsider?"

"We've already made the decision. I'm sorry. Please stay well and keep in touch."

"Bud, I think we should think through this. I have some stories in mind and was going to...."

But the line was dead. Bud had ended the call.

She dropped her folders and slummed on the couch. Her total savings were less than $2100 and her $1500 rent was due in a week. She dialed Brigid but remembered she was on vacation out west for the rest of the month.

Then he remembered Winger's Market was looking for clerk. Perhaps that might help for a while. She raced down to the market.

"Hello, you may remember me. Been in a couple times. Name's Shannon and I live up at Judge Benson's place."

"Yep, rememba.' Some folks were just in hereah 'bout you," Mabel said.

"Folks? About me? Who?"

Mabel walked to the bulletin board and removed the poster.

"Seems tha' dog is missin' again. Gone!"

Shannon pulled the poster from her. One of the photographs of Chauncey was the same one she had seen just the day before, a closeup of her face. She read it slowly.

"Oh God! Gone? Where?"

"Ran off somewhere down in Goshen town. Tha' woman thought she might be headed hereah, up to your place, bein' her former home and all."

"Woman? Who was that?"

"An older woman, grey hair, pulled back, thin gal. Mentioned the dog was hers. That Dru woman. Was with a man. Think his name was Dave."

"Dru? She's my landlady. I rent the old Benson's place up there."

"She figured the dog might be headed your way so you might want to put out some food or treats for it. Know you had bought some a while ago."

"Yes, that was for the neighbor's dog, Barney. Belongs to Jake Tollinger and his daughter."

"Yep, know Jake. Good friend."

Shannon stared at the poster. The thought of Chauncey lost in the woods overwhelmed her. She crouched down against the counter.

"You okay, Miss? Is it tha' dog?"

"Yes, but you don't understand. It's important...very important...we must find her."

"Not likely. When them dogs get lost in the woods, it's ova' for them much of the time. Was nearly before...the dog got tangled with some coyotes and a wolf, I heard. And she's older now...likely a goner now."

She dropped the poster and brought her hand to her face. Mabel put her hand on her shoulder.

"Why is tha' dog so important to you, Miss?"

Shannon didn't answer. She had forgotten about the job. She stood and without a word, walked out.

In the parking lot, Shannon sat alone in her car, her hands tightly gripping the steering wheel as she stared across the road to the forest's edge. She imagined Chauncey running through the thickets, racing from the woods and into the clearing. She could almost see it, just beyond her windshield, just right in front of her, not far away. She raised her hand. Just a sign to bring her out.

But the still autumn day remained unchanged.

She would never know it had been Jake Tollinger and his daughter Joannie who had sat in this very spot years earlier feeling the same agony of losing a dog. She slumped onto the steering wheel and began to weep.

At some point, not knowing whether it was the right time or not, she started the car and drove off, her heavy heart pounding.

It was not long before the real trouble started.

She skipped dinner and lay on her bed, again staring at the photographs. One, the closeup of Chauncey, had been on the poster at Winger's. She stared into the dog's eyes and imagined Chauncey lost and alone, in trouble, unable to help herself, crying for help. Her eyes fluttered. Her heart pounded in her chest.

She ran downstairs and out to the edge of the forest, crying for the dog.

"Chauncey! Chauncey! Come to me! Come, please come!"

She knelt in the tall grass, the photograph clenched in her hand, screaming into the trees.

"Chauncey, please come back. I need you!"

A massive rush of adrenaline shot through her. A sudden, intense pain filled her chest, crushing it under a massive weight. She clenched her breast and collapsed onto the grass.

Jake Tollinger was sitting in his upstairs bedroom, reading the newspaper when he heard the screams. They had come from Judge Benson's place. He looked out across Sarah Bristoll's yard and spotted someone lying in the far field. He called 9-1-1 and ran out.

It was nearly dark when the paramedics arrived.

Melony, the same paramedic that had seen Shannon only days earlier, knelt to woman.

"Shannon, can you hear me?"

Her eyes were rolled up.

Shannon's EKG was erratic and she couldn't breathe.

"You're having a cardiac arrest. A heart attack. We need to get you into the hospital. Stay with me! Stay awake, Shannon!"

At the Glenriver Regional Hospital, they were met by Dr. Chamborne, the lead cardiologist, the same doctor that had found Dirck Hansen a year earlier as he lay near death.

Shannon struggled to breathe. Gerald Chamborne fitted an oxygen mask and opened her blouse. He noticed her scar.

"Isn't this the same woman you called us about just a day or so ago, the one who they found under the shower, unconscious? Why didn't you bring her in then? She's in full cardiac arrest now!"

A loud voice signaled through the hospital corridors.

"Code Blue. Doctors Putnam and the Blue Team to ER. Code Blue!"

Two nurses and another doctor blasted through the ER doors.

"Tell me what you're feeling," Dr. Chamborne said.

Her eyes fluttered. She whispered.

"Heavy pain… chest. Can't breathe…arms hurt."

Her eyes closed and she went limp. A nurse handed Chamborne the defibrillator. He placed paddles on her chest.

"CLEAR!"

Shannon's body bolted up.

He brought a stethoscope to her breast. No response.

"CLEAR!"

A second shock nearly pulled her off the table.

"Have a heartbeat. Push IV fluids and nitro!"

Two nurses and doctors were bent over the woman.

"Can you hear my voice? Can you see me?"

Her eyes opened.

"Yes. Where?"

"In hospital. How long since you had heart surgery?"

"Year ago. Transplant. Heart going bad?"

"It's beating now. You had a heart attack. Were you doing something strenuous or something unusual?"

"No. Standing in a field."

"Ok, just rest quietly."

A large instrument was wheeled into the ER.

"We're going to take a picture of your heart with this camera, an echocardiogram. It'll tell us more. Just relax."

"The sonographer smeared gel on Shannon's chest and moved paddles across her left breastbone. The dark screen lit up with scrambled images in blue and orange. Her beating heart appeared.

Chamborne leaned into the moving image. The sonographer quietly pointed to an area and looked up at the cardiologist with raised eyebrows. He spoke softly.

"Enlarged left ventricle. Takotsubo cardiomyopathy. The muscle's weakened and can't pump. I've only seen this in simulated training."

Takotsubo, *octopus pot* in Japanese, was the name given to the heart muscle shaped oddly like the Japanese fishing pot. It had a narrow neck and a rounded bottom. Dr. Chamborne had seen it once in a middle-aged woman who had suddenly lost her husband. During the extreme stress, adrenaline stuns the heart, changes the heart muscle, and prevents the ventricle from contracting. The ventricle balloons. And it occurs only in women.

But from Chamborne's medical training, it was just called "broken-heart syndrome."

"Shannon. Tell me what happened to you before this happened. Was there some family dispute or did you lose something valuable like a family member?"

She stared at the doctor.

"Lost dog."

"Was the dog a therapy or service dog of yours?"

"I just need…the dog. Lost. Gone. Maybe dead," she said in short breaths. She struggled to sit up.

"You need to rest now. I am in touch with your cardio team at Dana Farber in Boston. Patricia Tatters and Chris Davis. We will be speaking with them since they were your transplant docs.

"Oh God…am I going to…lose my heart? What will happen?"

"Your heart is beating okay for now but you need to stay quiet and let the medicines work. Our team will monitor you today and through the night. You'll be here for at least another day."

Shannon's EKG, echocardiogram, blood workup was sent electronically to Dana Farber. Chris Davis and Patricia Tatters called Gerald Chamborne that early evening.

Dr. Tatters looked at the heart images on a screen.

"Gerald, we need to get Miss Murphy down here to Boston tomorrow. This enlarged ventricle worries me. I've seen a few instances of takotsubo cardiomyopathy. Usually it's seen in patients who receive a shock of bad news or an unexpected loss. Her EKG looks like a typical heart attack but the echo image shows the ballooning ventricle. And her blood biomarker, the troponin, show the muscle has been stunned. It's weakened. She needs treatment with beta blockers and diuretics. Patients recover in about a month or two but over a quarter of them have heart failure after this. We have a dedicated unit for these cases."

"I'll arrange for our team to prep her for the heliopad and 'coper ride down to Boston first thing tomorrow," Chamborne said.

"Did you find out what could have triggered this? She was healthy at her checkups and her life and family seemed stable."

"She told me it was about some dog. Maybe her dog died. I couldn't get any more out of her."

"Right. I think we need to check on the donor. Perhaps there's a clue in there somewhere. Thanks Gerald."

Throughout her long and uneasy night in the hospital room, nurses kept hearing the woman whispering *Chauncey*.

21

Something cold at her face woke her. Chauncey opened her eyes to a fawn nibbling at her muzzle. She lifted her head and licked its cheek, sending it skirting awkwardly back to the safety of its forest home.

She then remembered where she was. Not home, not with Dru or Callie at CAS but again, deep in the forests, lost and alone. It was early morning and still dark.

She pulled in the air. The familiar smell was there but faint. She straightened herself out from her warm bed, shook off the leaves and moss, and ran forward. It was the second day and she knew it would take at least two more days to reach the scent.

She raced into the unknown, callous to her mounting pain and hunger. The smell drove her beyond that which pulled her down. The forest was dark and from the valley below, far-off howls of wolves echoed through the trees. She continued forward.

The old man had to sit down. He had been out here in the woods for over an hour this early morning. At nearly eighty, his body just wouldn't cooperate like it once had, despite his nearly fifty years of hunting and hiking here, his home. He lay his gun and pack onto a rock and stretched out his aching legs. The light had just broken from the far ridge and the forest was quiet this time of day. He knew the big hunters, the wolves and bears, even the smaller coyotes, would be asleep. Only deer and rabbits would be foraging. But as he quieted down, he heard far-off sounds of growling and yipping, grunting. Unexpected sounds. Wolves! He jumped up and moved towards the commotion.

A quarter of a mile in, he reached a ridge overlooking a narrow valley. Through the dense firs and brush, he saw two large creatures circling rapidly about, their guttural sounds unmistakable. Grey wolves. Amidst the growling, he heard a loud bark and a cry, not that of wolves. He cocked his loaded gun and moved forward. Two male wolves spotted him, their gold diabolical eyes fixing on the old man. The larger wolf circled around, revealing another creature lying in the bush behind it. He couldn't quite make it out but could see it was their intended meal.

"Away! Out!" he yelled and waved his arms.

A smaller wolf turned its head away from the prey and joined his partner as the new threat approached them. The old man raised his rifle and fired. The loud blast exploded over the wolves and they scattered to safety. But the man knew their prey was valuable and this would only momentarily deter them.

As he descended into the valley, he saw a blonde dog lying in the thicket, its back leg trapped in a tangle of twigs wound around a tree trunk. The dog was crying, its trapped leg flailing as it desperately tried to get free. The hunter approached carefully, trying not to alarm the dog who looked up at the man, great fear radiating from its eyes.

He crouched down.

"There, there. It's okay, now. Let me help you out, little pup."

He laid his rife down and smoothed his hand across the dog's back to quell its fear. She buried her head into the man's arm and whined. He carefully untangled its trapped leg and rubbed it to feel if it had been broken. It hadn't.

The shaking dog climbed onto the man. He stroked her thick fur. He could see it was not an old dog, but not young either, and judging by its well-cut and brushed coat, likely someone's pet. It wore a collar that read *Chauncey/CAS*.

"Is that your name, pup? Chaun-cey? What's *CAS* mean?"

Chauncey shivered as he stroked her. She was safe now. The man knew her name and was kind. She knew he would help her.

"What you doin' out here in these woods, friend? You ought not be out here, little pup."

She relaxed as he rubbed her back.

He emptied his bag of nuts into his hand. She lapped up the food. It wasn't anything she had ever tasted, but she was famished and it tasted good. The hunter once had had a dog of his own and knew this was no place for a dog.

But that was not primarily on his mind. He knew the wolves would be back and they would catch her if she ran. He pulled a rope from his pack and gently placed it around her neck and tied the end to a tree. He picked up his rifle and stood.

He scanned the dense pines.

The larger wolf had been half hidden by a thicket and reappeared. It walked cautiously towards him. Its blood-stained muzzle was wrinkled, revealing its razor fangs. It advanced slowly, almost in a friendly manner, but he knew better.

"Back!" the man yelled.

He stepped forward, his gun at the ready.

The wolf stopped. It was twenty feet away from him and the dog crouching behind him. He had seen wolves before but not this close. The animal was stark and foreign yet beautiful and sleek. The wolf froze, unafraid, its long muscular legs shivering as it considered the threat, wanting desperately to reach the dog.

The wolf crept slowly forward. It was now close enough for a strike. Its thick grey pelt was raised and it crouched low and forward, its shoulder blades protruding, ready to pounce.

The man's trigger finger tightened.

"Not one more step!"

The wolf's head lowered and his large body shook.

The gun fired. An enormous blast exploded just over the wolf's head, flipping the creature backward like a limp doll. It yelped loudly and righted itself, slinking back to its woodland home like a frightened dog, its pride the only damage. The other wolf was nowhere to be seen.

The man turned back to the shivering dog. He felt her flank and felt ribs. He knew the dog was starving and he emptied another packet of walnuts into his palm. She devoured them and looked up at him for more.

"That's it, youngster. You're needing some attention and real food. You come with me back to my place. It's not far, just over that ridge. Not far, good dog, let's go."

He motioned her to follow. Chauncey knew she couldn't make it any longer and the man was kind and would help her.

She followed him.

The man was Malcolm Longridge, who lived miles from any Vermont towns in a small stone house that had been in his family for two generations. He was a tall, austerely pleasant man, a writer by profession and the author of natural history of his home state of Vermont. Hunting was a past-time and he trapped rabbits for the meat that he occasionally enjoyed as winter approached. Deer or other large game were off limits as they were his woodland friends, and he carried a gun only for protection from the wolves and bears. To trap rabbits, he used a humane trap, his own invention. To bait it, he would pour a cup of his freshly made hard apple cider into a dish at the end a small open cage. The strong apple scent would lure the rabbit and, as the animal lapped up the delicious sweet liquid, they would slowly pass out from intoxication and the strength of the alcohol would gently euthanize the animal. He knew the animals wouldn't panic or feel pain but only pleasure of what would be their first and only drunken experience, and he would find them lying in the trap, seemingly asleep. But still, Malcolm didn't even like doing this and only for necessity took six or seven rabbits in winter. He was relieved had hadn't caught any in the past day.

But this morning, he had greater things on his mind. His new companion needed help.

It took them half hour to reach his cabin. It was a one bedroom stone house with a galley kitchen. He lit a fire to warm the room. Chauncey lay exhausted on the large worn rug in the living room, curiously watching Malcolm move about the galley. The smells of the cooking food overwhelmed her. A large metal bowl was set before her filled with cooked eggs, day-old sausages, pieces of warmed rabbit meat, carrots, cabbage.

She dove into the food. It was gone before Malcolm could look back. She stood over the bowl, her tail swinging wildly.

"Bet that was good, wasn't it, Chaun-cey? Want more?"

She loved hearing her name called even though he pronounced it funny. A weak bark answered.

By early afternoon, with two generous bowlfuls of food and fresh water in her warm belly, Chauncey slept by the crackling fire in Malcom Longridge's cabin. It was peaceful here, the only sound rising from the occasional crackling logs or the creaking of Malcolm's wooden rocking chair as he sat nearby, considering his new friend.

"Guess we have to find out who you are, Chaun-cey, don't we dear?" he cooed to her.

But Malcolm Longridge wasn't anxious to part with his new

companion. He lived alone and normally enjoyed having the house to himself, especially during his creative periods when he would write. But it had only been a year ago that he had lost his most trusted and dear companion of fourteen years, a black Flat-Coated Retriever named "Jasper," a dog he had raised as a puppy, a dog who had given him daily joy for so many years, and he sorely missed his sweet Jasper. That, and Malcolm would turn eighty this winter and the recent years had brought a deep loneliness he hadn't before experienced. Companionship was everything to him now.

Malcolm wasn't able to care for the house like he had in his earlier years and recently enjoyed a simple arrangement with Mrs. Finley and her partner Silas, an older couple who lived a quarter mile across the field in their small cabin. Bernice or "Bernie" Finley came by twice a week to clean and look after Malcom's home and Silas took care of the aging furnace and the many odd jobs that the old stone house required.

Today was Bernie's cleaning day.

A familiar knock was heard. Chauncey raised her heavy head.

"Malcom? You home?" Bernie said as she opened the door.

"Yep. Forgot about today. Come on in. Careful, got a new friend in here."

Chauncey was at the door, her tail swinging wildly. The woman bent forward and gently stroked her muzzle.

"Well, hello, sweet thing. Who are you then?"

"That's Chauncey. Found her this mornin' in the woods. Poor pooch had gotten tangled and a couple of those wolves wanted her for breakfast. Took her in. Poor dog was famished and exhausted."

Mrs. Finley sat on the floor, smoothing her hands across the dog's face.

"Caught in the woods? Wolves? That's a stroke a-luck you found her. She's a sweet one. Looks like a pet. Any ideas?"

"Not one. Unusual for a dog to be out there. From her looks, bet she'd been out in those woods for a time, maybe a week or so. Probably lost. Don't know anyone around here that's missing a dog, do you?"

"No, but Silas mentioned he had heard some rumor about a valuable dog goin' missing down in Goshen way but that's a-ways away from hereah."

"Can't imagine a dog coming up here that far. Doesn't seem likely. She needs rest. Now that I have this hungry dog, can you pick up some groceries for me at Mac's? Don't want to leave the dog here alone. I'll make a list."

"Yep. I'll grab what you need and get back hereah later. Silas went up East Burke way for supplies. Maybe someone up theyah or over at Mac's might know about her."

The closing door didn't rouse Chauncey who was stretched back out in front of the fire.

As Malcolm watched over her, Chauncey slept by the fire all that day and into the evening. The familiar smells that had swirled in her brain had now dissipated, giving her much-needed peace.

22

Shannon woke to see the doctor standing by her bedside. She had arrived at Dana Farber Cardiac Ward an hour before and Dr. Davis had received her report from Dr. Patricia Tatters.

"Shannon, you had us worried up there in Vermont. We've gone over your echocardiogram and blood tests. You had a significant heart attack. Can you tell me more about what happened right before that?" Davis said.

She was still groggy from the sedatives. She looked at the man but couldn't remember his name.

"Before then? I don't remember, doctor. I was at outside my home when I remember this sudden crushing pain in my chest. I felt stunned, like my heart was breaking."

"Yes, you had a stress-induced cardiomyopathy. In the trade, we call it "broken heart syndrome." Happens after a severe emotional stress. Did a family member pass away?"

She frowned.

"Lost a dog. Need to find it."

She tried to sit up.

"You need to stay quiet and rest. Is the dog your therapy or service dog?"

Shannon struggled to sit up.

"It's important. We need to find her."

"Okay, we'll talk more about it later. We'll need more tests. The main thing is for you to rest."

Down the hall in the cardiac imaging lab, a team of doctors and nurses examined Shannon Murphy's heart images on two large screens. Dr. Davis sat in the center of them, looking at one image. There was a long silence before he sat back.

"This isn't looking positive. Take a look at this right ultrasound image. That's clear takotsubo cardiopathy. The way that ventricle has enlarged, it won't contract right. And here, these restricted vessels. And troponin and c-reactive protein levels are both off."

Dr. Burke had seen this before in a patient at the Cleveland Clinic. He shook his head.

"It looks almost like the heart being rejected. But this is now a year out and I've never seen anything like this so late after transplant. We need to put her into a strict anti-rejection protocol."

Christopher Davis typed the orders and protocol into the Starflight System, a database of patient records agnostic to patient identification.

As he typed, an encrypted message appeared across the bottom of the screen. It was from UNOS. He clicked on it.

To: Christopher H. Davis, MD.

From: United Network for Organ Sharing Database.

Re: Requested record.

Patient Shannon Marie Murphy, 50-year-old female heart transplant recipient.

Identity of donor: Mr. Dirck Hansen, 3982 Route 44, Glenriver, Vermont. No additional data available. END

Davis switched to another screen entitled PATIENT DATABASE SEARCH and typed in DIRCK HANSEN, GLENRIVER, VERMONT.

Pages of information appeared on the screen. He scrolled through them in silence. They listed man's age, height and weight, and medical history.

He scrolled to the bottom and stopped.

It read:

Dirck Hansen, a decorated war hero (Captain, Iraqi Freedom Campaign 2003-2005), was diagnosed with severe PTSD in 2005 and was matched with a service dog. The service dog registered to Canines Assisting Soldiers, Baker's Mills, NY, is a female Golden Retriever named 'Chauncey'. END

At the bottom of the text was a photograph of Dirck Hansen standing in his green Army uniform, a handsome blonde dog by his side.

The doctor sat back in his chair staring at the screen. There was a long silence. He shook his head.

"Shannon Murphy received Dirck Hansen's heart. And his dog, 'Chauncey' must have meant everything to the veteran. You know, it's quite rare but many years ago, my chief mentor once told me about a transplant recipient, a woman, who had taken on the heart donor's persona…their worries, their guilt, their feelings, their losses. Could it be possible that Shannon…."

He reached over and typed into google search **Dirck Hansen dog Chauncey**.

The screen flashed with three headlines:

-FAMOUS SERVICE DOG OF DIRCK HANSEN STILL MISSING
-CAS SEARCHING FOR THERAPY DOG 'CHAUNCEY'
-THERAPY DOG FEARED DEAD AFTER A WEEK LOST

The last one caught his attention.

"Oh, this is troubling. The veteran's service dog is missing, says here perhaps dead. Looks like it had belonged to this organization, Canine Assisting Soldiers. Is it possible that Shannon had taken on Dirck Hansen's persona after receiving his heart and her attack was precipitated by news that the dog had gone missing or died? This would explain the symptoms of 'broken heart' syndrome. I can't think of what else might have caused this."

"I've never heard of that...the recipient taking on the donor's persona and reacting like that...about a dog?" Dr. Burke said.

"Well, we must to keep this to ourselves. It could worsen her condition if she knew. As the recipient, she wasn't allowed to know the donor's identity. I'll get ahold of the dog place and let them know about this. But right now, we need to get her into therapy tomorrow. This information stays in this room."

In the coming weeks, Shannon was placed on a restricted diet and given daily anti-rejection drugs, some of which made her worse. She underwent physical therapy that strained her body to a breaking point. Brigid traveled to Boston and rented one of the hospital-provided apartments. The staff kept them both away from the computer and the internet for fear that they would find more news about the dog Shannon kept talking about.

Nobody knew where Chauncey was and some reports speculated that the dog had died.

And despite Shannon's intensive treatment, her condition grew worse.

23

After not answering her phone or paying last month's rent, Dru drove to Judge Benson's place.

She knocked on the kitchen door. There was no answer but Shannon's Subaru was still parked by the garage. She glanced down and noticed the note lying in the bushes, water-logged from the recent rains. It had been there over a week. She knew something had happened to the woman.

"Oh girl, where would Shannon have gone?" she said to Callie who also sensed something wrong.

Dru had brought Callie in hopes she might pick up Chauncey's sent. She pulled out her house keys but noticed the door was ajar.

An intruder? What if someone had broken in and hurt the woman. She called out.

"Who's there? Show yourself!"

Although she had been out of the service for over forty years, she was still a Marine and her training had taught her how to eliminate any threat.

She stepped in quietly.

"Shannon, are you there?"

Callie broke free and raced up the stairs.

"Careful, girl!"

She ran upstairs to the bedroom where Callie had run. The bed was unmade and pillows and blankets were strewn about with dozens of photographs of Dirck and Chauncey. Dru had not seen them before. She noticed an opened safe inside one of the side walls.

"Looks like he had kept some of these to himself," she said to her dog.

Callie was wandering around the room smelling the chairs and floor, whining lightly.

"What do you smell, girl? Something important here?"

She went to the downstairs bedroom that Shannon was using as an office. In the small typewriter, a partially typed page protruded. It read:

When Grover's Corner Feedstore caught fire, it was said that old man Grover had gotten trapped inside the blaze but a ghost dog had run in after him and dragged him to safety in the field in front. Grover never saw the dog after that night. Years later, it showed up again, according to Grace and Lucy Matters as it appeared in the night and sat in the field across from their house. Stories about the dog surfaced and people claimed to have seen it but dog remained elusive, mostly recounted in stories at town meetings and sewing circles.

Then, more recently, there was speculation that the dog had come back to life as a service dog who belonged to the retired Army Captain Dirck Hansen who lived in Judge Benson's homestead. The dog was a young beautiful Golden Retriever named Chauncey.

Chauncey Chauncey Chauncey Chauncey

She pulled the paper free and re-read it in disbelief. Why was Shannon so fixed on her dog and how had she found all those photographs that even she didn't know about? She called Dave Ballard but there was no answer. She was punching in the number for CAS when her phone beeped and flashed *Unknown Caller.*

"Dru Vaughn here."

"Mrs. Vaughn? My name is Christopher Davis, a physician at the Dana Farber Hospital in Boson. I hope I'm not disturbing."

"Dr. Davis? I don't know a Dr. Davis. How did you get my number and name?"

"I am the chief cardiologist here at Dana Farber. The people at your organization CAS gave me your name and number."

"Does this have to do with our lost dog, Chauncey?"

"Well, not directly, but yes. I don't know if you know Shannon Murphy. She is under my care here in the cardiac ward."

"Cardiac ward? Boston? My God, what happened?"

"Miss Murphy had a significant cardiac arrest several days ago in Vermont and was airlifted to our facility from Glenriver Hospital. She is in intensive care."

"Oh God! I was afraid something had happened to her. I'm her landlady and right now, I'm at the house she rents here in Glenriver, Vermont."

"The paramedics found her out in the field behind the house she rents."

"Up here?"

"The report says she was picked up at 3982 Route 44 in Glenriver. Is that where you are?"

"Yes, that's my house. But you say she was in a field?"

"Yes, out behind the house, in a field. She mentioned to the paramedics something about losing a dog. And we investigated how her heart attack might be related to this."

"A dog? What dog?"

"We wondered the same thing. Shannon Murphy had been dying of heart failure well over a year ago and was the recipient of a heart transplant. We just learned that her donor was Dirck Hansen, a veteran who lived there in Glenriver. He lived at that address. Do you know Mr. Hansen?"

Dru dropped the phone and fell to her knees. She couldn't catch her breath.

"Miss Vaughn, are you there? Are you okay?"

She picked up the phone.

"Dr. Davis. You say Shannon Murphy received Dirck Hansen's heart? Did I hear that right?"

"Yes. We confirmed that from the national organ sharing organization, UNOS. It had been about a year ago and she had been doing quite well as a transplant recipient. That is until her cardiac arrest. We also learned that Dirck Hansen had a service dog named "Chauncey" and that the dog was under care at CAS, your organization, until it went missing a week ago. Can you tell me about that?"

"After Mr. Hansen died, Chauncey went back to me and my training group in New York. She's now a therapy dog. Over two weeks ago, she ran away at the Goshen VA Hospital in Vermont. We have been intensely searching for her and have been up here, hoping she'd come back to her old home. I own the house now. It was Dirck Hansen's house. It's where Shannon Murphy lives. But I can't understand…."

Her mind was racing through the story but she couldn't comprehend what had happened. Shannon had Dirck's heart!

"Well, I've been trying to understand why she had this heart attack. Her heart symptoms were identical to those we call takotsubo cardiomyopathy, in Japanese, called an "octopus pot"—it's the name given to the heart muscle shaped oddly like the narrow-necked pot. It's a serious condition in which the ventricle balloons out."

"Tako…I'm afraid I don't follow."

"I'm sorry. It's also known as *broken-heart syndrome.* Happens in female patients that suffer severe emotional stress like the sudden loss of a loved one. We found it significant that Shannon Murphy had received Dirck Hansen's heart. In rare cases, the heart recipient can take on the persona of the donor. Like Mr. Hansen. We thought it possible that Miss Murphy reacted to the loss of Chauncey just like Dirck Hansen would have. We must assume she found out about the missing dog, and some speculated that Chauncey was feared dead."

"Take on Dirck's persona…."

Dru stared out the window, thinking about Dirck and the intense grief he had experienced years ago when his dog had been stolen. It nearly had killed him.

"Is Shannon going to be okay? How serious is this?"

"Well, time will tell. But her symptoms mimic heart rejection—it happens when the heart recipient rejects the heart they receive. We're treating her for that but the outcome is not certain. I needed to understand her state of mind to guide her treatment any further."

"Dirck Hansen was close to me. Very close. I helped train and pair the Chauncey to Dirck as a PTSD service dog. We're both veterans. That dog had been his savior. Literally. Without her, he would have died," she said.

Her voice was trembling.

"I understand. We think Dirck's heart is telling Shannon this, and she somehow found out the dog was lost or feared dead, which is what we think caused this severe reaction."

Even Christopher Davis was having a difficult time believing what he was telling the woman but he couldn't come up with anything else.

"So, the loss she's experiencing is from the loss of Chauncey?"

"We think so. It's unusual but we think the broken heart symptoms might be from the loss of the dog that Dirck would have experienced."

"Will she survive otherwise?"

“It’s uncertain. Most patients who have such a serious reaction don’t recover unless the loss is resolved.”

Dru was stunned. She was staring out to the field.

“Dr. Davis, can I get your number down there? I need some time to absorb this, to try and come up with some way to help.”

“Yes, you can get ahold of me on a page by dialing 1248149227 and punch in my pager number 99022.”

Dru ended the call. Callie was crying loudly at the kitchen door. she opened it and the dog raced out through the backyard and into the far field. She ran after her.

“What do you see, girl?”

Callie was in the field, zig-zagging about, tracing the ground with her nose.

The tall summer grasses had dried and in one spot, a large section was bent over. In the shape of a body. Medical tape was scattered about.

Callie lay onto the spot and looked up at her.

“My God, this is where she fell! Could Dirck’s heart inside her be breaking from the loss of Chauncey?”

She knelt onto the grassy outline of Shannon’s body and wrapped her arm around Callie.

“We must find Chauncey, girl! We must!”

24

At Ruby Lee's Store in East Burke, Silas had heard rumors about a lost dog way down in Goshen but in the middle of the previous night, farmer Johnson's 16-year-old daughter had run off with an out-of-town boy and nobody was talking about a lost dog. And Silas was in a hurry to get home—there was also talk about a large nor'easter running up the coast, promising a big storm. And local Vermonters were the best predictors of weather. He left for home.

"Got the part for the Longridge stove and tha' good cheese you like," Silas said as he set down the bags in Mrs. Finley's kitchen. "Saw post a-some lost dog down in Goshen way but didn't have no picture on it and don' think it's up this a-way. But tha' dog was a special one. Some therapy dog or service one I read."

"We'll Malcolm's pretty fond of that dog he found. We'll not mention anything 'bout a lost dog. He'd do well with a companion at his age. Was tough on him losin' his Jasper. He loved that pooch so," Bernie said.

That afternoon, she picked up supplies at Mac's store and went back to Malcolm's cabin. She needed to get back before the snows came through.

Chauncey jumped to Bernie as she opened the door.

"There, there, little one. You like that smell on my hands? Been bakin' a cake for Silas."

They unpacked the groceries.

"Yeah, she's been sleeping good for a while now. Seems to like it here and sure likes my meals I make for her. Just like my Jasper. He used to love cooked eggs and sausage. Think I'll throw in some of that yoghurt I got from the Bradford farm last week."

Chauncey was staring intently at Malcolm in anticipation of the yoghurt.

"Well Silas jus' got back from in East Burke. No mention of any dog goin' lost. They would know and I saw nothin' in Macs."

But she but hadn't noticed the posters in the back post board in Macs and the two tacked outside the local church.

"Can't imagine why she was alone in the woods. She's got that collar with her name but no idea of what "CAS" means. Maybe her initials…Chauncey something."

"Well, keep her safe. I'll be back early next week to clean, probably Tuesday mornin'."

It was 4 p.m., and he prepared cooked rabbit and vegetables. For them both. Topped with yoghurt. He laughed as he watched his dog dance about the kitchen. He remembered well how joyful his Jasper had been at dinnertime, even in her last few months, and watching Chauncey greatly lifted his spirits. He crouched down, stroking her back as she inhaled large chunks of rabbit. She collapsed by the bowl, happy.

He put his hands on her head. He was beginning to dearly love this dog and would keep her if they couldn't find her owner. But he wasn't looking.

While Malcom slept by his dog that night, a snowstorm descended onto the land, silently and heavily. The nor'easter was larger than even the locals predicted, and by 5 a.m., three feet of snow had blanketed Malcolm Longridge's stone house, his fence and walls, the surrounding meadows and fields, and all the meadows, creeks, and rivers throughout Vermont. Only snowshoes could get through.

A muffled thump woke Chauncey. It was 6 a.m. She raised her head up to Malcolm who was still snoring in the small bed next to her. She walked to the window and jumped up to the sill. The window was nearly obscured by snowdrifts and everything was white. She slowly took in a breath and held it, trying to recapture the smell that had brought her here, but the snow had obscured even the faintest smells. She leapt up onto Malcolm's bed.

"Ooof! Whaaa…oh, hello sweet girl! Good to see you, too. You sleep good?"

Chauncey stretched across him and licked his chin. She was ready for breakfast. Malcolm slowly dragged his achy body out of the warm bed and lit a fire. He pulled the curtain aside.

"Oh lord-y! That's one big snow. Looks like feet out there. Still comin' down, too. Glad we have plenty of supplies and wood, girl. Nobody getting' in or out now. Hope that's okay with you."

She pranced to the front door and whined.

"Time to do your business?"

He opened the door. Snow had obscured the porch stairs and even drifted up to the front door but Chauncey was undeterred. She pushed through the thick mounds down the stairs and squatted. Malcolm watched as she panted lightly, only her head and shoulders visible. She smiled at him.

"Do your business, girl. We'll see about getting you out later. I know you like this stuff. Just like my Jasper."

She wiggled out of her snow rut and struggled back onto the porch. Halfway to the door, she turned back towards the white-covered woods.

She was after something out there, and Malcolm knew it.

"Still lookin' for your owners, girl? Where might they be? They would surely be looking for you," he said but knew nobody would be out in this deep snow.

Malcolm could see his dog was unsettled. Chauncey stood motionless, her blonde fur covered in white. She scanned the white landscape again and once she was satisfied there were no trace of any smells, she snorted a breath and turned back to the warm cottage.

Callie shifted on the couch, waking Dru. It was now dark and she went to the kitchen and turned on the porch lights. Outside, snow descended heavily, obscuring the field where she and Callie had just been that morning. It looked like a large storm and she'd have to stay put.

She tried Dave again. But it didn't answer and got forwarded.

"CAS. Jessica speaking," the woman said.

"Jessie, it's Dru. Has Dave checked in?"

"No, he's out with the search party down near Goshen. But imagine they may have given up with this snow. It's bad here and know it's up your way too."

"I need to reach him. Can you call Maggie? I don't have her number. See if she can reach him. I'm here at the Judge Benson place and have to spend the night with this storm."

"I'll call her but the reception isn't great anywhere."

"Any word on Chauncey? Anything?"

"No, the teams have been in touch with Dave but we haven't heard anything yet. I hope she isn't stuck in this snow. She'll never make it."

"Don't worry. She's a strong girl," Dru said but as she looked out at the thickening snow, her heart sunk.

"Just call me when you get Dave. Make sure he calls right away. Very important."

She ended the call and walked through the house, turning on lights. She checked the refrigerator. Carrots, cucumbers, eggs, some bread. She remembered Shannon had been on a restricted diet. She sliced vegetables and added eggs and cheese and bread and fed Callie while she sat in the kitchen watching the snow descend.

She wasn't hungry after receiving the news about Shannon.

"Sorry, girl. Not much tonight."

They went to the upstairs bedroom and looked out the picture window. The porch lights illuminated the snow but she barely could see the white field beyond in the dim light. She imagined Chauncey somewhere in the storm, struggling to find Shannon. She looked down at Callie.

"That's what she's been after. Chauncey must have smelled Shannon when she was in that field and must be headed up this way," she said to her dog.

But Shannon was now in Boston and Chauncey could never find her scent that far away.

Dru lay on the bed with Callie. The photographs were still scattered about. She looked at the images of Dirck and Chauncey.

"She must sense Dirck in Shannon, Callie. She knows he's alive in her!"

The dog's warm eyes surveyed her worried face.

"You know it too, girl. You'll help me find Chauncey. She's out there somewhere."

She closed her eyes, the dog in her lap. The silent snows drifted onto the land. Hours past.

The vibration woke her. She struggled to find her phone.

"Dru, is that you?" Dave Ballard said.

She hadn't answered.

"Oh...Dave...sorry, I was asleep. We're stuck out here at Judge Benson's place."

"Tried last night but service was out. Storm's bad. We are snowbound here in Goshen. We were out looking for her until it got bad and barely made it back."

"Any word, anything?"

"Nothing, Dru. Really worried about our girl in this storm. Pretty unusual for the late fall and it's wet snow so it's tough getting through."

"I came out here because rent wasn't paid and phone calls went unanswered. Got a call from a doctor at the Farber cardiac hospital in Boson. Shannon was taken there. She had a heart attack, apparently right out here in the field."

"Heart attack?"

"Dave—this is going to be hard to take in—but the doctor told me that Shannon had been a heart recipient. She had been dying of heart failure over a year ago and she got a heart transplant."

"Oh, is that what caused the heart attack? Will she be okay?"

"Dave—Shannon Murphy received Dirck Hansen's heart!"

There was silence on the line.

"They confirmed it. Dirck was an organ donor, I now remember that. And his heart went to Shannon."

"What? My God, that's…."

"Yes. That's the reason Shannon was drawn so strongly to this place, this house, the reason Callie was so attracted to her. I found photographs of Dirck and Chauncey here I didn't even know they existed. She must have known they were here."

"That's why Chauncey took off. She's after Shannon! She must have smelled her or sensed her somehow. Is that possible?"

"The doctor thinks that she may have taken on some of Dirck, his personality, feelings, fears. And especially, the love of Chauncey. It lives within her heart. She must have found out that

Chauncey was missing. Our posters are all over Glenriver. Surely she must have seen one."

"I can't get my head around this, Dru."

"They found her lying in the field and they took her to Glenriver hospital and then down to Boston. The doctor said her heart attack was caused by something called *broken-heart syndrome.*"

"My God, then Chauncey must be headed up there after her."

"Yes, she likely would have but Shannon's down in Boston now. Her scent's too far away."

"Okay, I'm coming up to you. We'll get a team to start looking. I'll drive the big Jeep. It'll get through anything and plows are out."

"Ok, I'll begin looking at first light. Seem to remember that Dirck had some old snowshoes somewhere. I'll take Callie with me, but the drifts are pretty big."

"Ok, keep your phone charged. I'll call later."

Dru looked out the window. At least the plow truck had cleared the driveway but they would have to wait until morning.

She woke at 6 a.m. and went to the garage. Behind old rotting wall barnboards hung Dirck's snowshoes. He had often used them when he took Chauncey into the deeper snows. She remembered how she loved to leap through the deep drifts as she followed him. The thought made her smile. But this stuff was deep and her dog was older now.

She cooked eggs and cheese for her and Callie, packed the remaining food, and set out with Callie. She knew Chauncey would be coming up from the south.

The morning temperature had risen to forty and her jacket would be enough. She put on snowshoes and fastened Callie's harness. They headed across the street, south into the Jackson's field and into the woods beyond.

No matter the dangers, she was determined to find Chauncey.

The snows continued to fall steadily throughout Vermont.

25

Both man and dog were nearly obscured in deep snow as they trudged the woodland paths, the only moving creatures in the silent stillness as the sun rose steadily over the distant hills.

Malcolm wouldn't go far, just far enough for Chauncey to stretch her legs and enjoy rolling in the snow. She had whined at the door all morning, begging for an outing.

They followed an old path that only Malcolm knew.

Here in the woods, the snows were not as deep, having been caught by the tall firs. Still, trudging with snowshoes was slow going, especially at Malcom's age. Chauncey was just happy to be outside again.

"You're just like Jasper. He loved this snow. I see it suits you, too," he said out of breath.

It had been nearly two years since he had been in the woods with a dog. The winter before she left him, Jasper had fallen ill with cancer and all Malcolm could do was comfort his ailing dog through his last days. It had been the worst day of his life when he took his last breath lying next to him on his bed. The pain never left him. But as he watched the energized dog leap through the deep snow, he felt the lingering misery easing from him.

It was noon and the temperatures had risen enough for Malcolm to take off his heavy coat and hat. He had gone further than he had planned and had grown tired. He rested against a tree trunk and pulled out his canteen. Chauncey climbed on his lap.

"Yeah, girl, this isn't far from where I found you tangling with those wolves. You were a lucky dog that day. Lucky for me too. We make a good pair, you and I."

He closed his eyes, Chauncey lying on his chest. They slept together in the heavy stillness of the forest.

They were sixty miles south of Glenriver.

An hour past.

From the north, a gust of wind across them. Chauncey's eyes opened and she pulled in the air.

A scent of Dru. And of Callie!

In a decisive moment, she bolted from the sleeping man as if he weren't even there.

She ran into the forest, leaping through the thick snow like a panicked animal.

By the time Malcolm could comprehend what had happened, his dog was well away from him, running north up a hill. He stumbled to his feet.

"Chauncey! Chauncey! Come back!" he yelled but knew it was of no use.

She had disappeared into the forest and there was no going after her at his age. He knew whatever had put her here in the first place was what she was now after.

"Probably home," he said under his breath as he stared at the still white landscape.

"Go home, girl. Go on home."

He loved that dog Chauncey. It felt like losing his Jasper all over again.

Dru had been moving at a strong pace all morning but trudging through snow in the old large snowshoes was difficult and they were both sapped.

She stopped and yelled out.

"Chauncey! Chauncey!"

Her cries echoed through the valley but were met with silence.

It was nearly 5 p.m. They had already traveled nearly forty miles. The sun had just disappeared over the far ridge. The nights would be near freezing and they'd have to find shelter. She decided to make camp.

She dug into the snows to find leaves and twigs and built a bed for them both. She built a large fire and they had eggs and cheese with apples and settled in for the night. She gave it one last try.

"Chauncey!" she yelled into the darkness.

Her voice echoed through the trees. It was met with *hoooooo who-hoooooo who-hoooo*, the far-off calls of the Vermont barred owls cooing to one other. She remembered that Dirck once told her the cries sounded like *who cooks for you?* She smiled at the thought.

Callie sat next to her by the fire, looking about, wondering what the new adventure would bring. The snows had stopped and they slept off and on through the night, broken only by Dru throwing more kindling on their fire.

By the time she had run nearly five miles, Chauncey was again exhausted. She stopped on a ridge and looked out. It was midafternoon. The smells were stronger now and directly in front of her. Distinctly Dru and Callie. Now, a trace of Dirck mixed in. She pressed forward across the field, but the snows had drifted there, forcing her to leap through them like a jackrabbit.

Despite her fatigue, she pressed forward, the smells her only compass north.

By late afternoon, she reached the far edge of the woods and stopped. Here, the landscape looked familiar, smelled familiar. She had been here before, it seemed. It strengthened her resolve.

But now it was nearly dark and had grown cold and she was exhausted. She scanned the forest for anything to give her shelter. The forest was home to all sorts of odd configurations of downed trees, stumps, piled leaves, but she had waited too long and it was now nearly impossible to make out enough details.

She came upon what looked like a large mound in the snow with a dark opening, perhaps a hollowed-out log. She crept forward and poked her nose into it. A rank smell filled her nose. Perhaps a dead animal or rotting food. But she was spent and needed to sleep somewhere safe. She crawled into the opening. It was pitch black and strangely warm inside. She curled up and laid down.

She fell into a deep sleep.

In the middle of the night, something next to her shifted. Something huge. She heard a low groan, a deep and heavy grumbling. Light from the faint distant moon had caught the edge of the snows and cast a dim blue glow about her. She tried to focus on what was next to her.

Then she saw it.

Inches from her was the face of an enormous black bear, its small half-opened eyes lazily gazing into darkness about it. It was a mother, fat and complacent in its early winter hibernation.

Chauncey's first instinct was to bolt and jump out but she knew upsetting the creature would be dangerous. And she was exhausted and perhaps the sleeping bear might let her borrow its den for the night, just to get warm for a few hours.

But the mother had other ideas. She had birthed just one cub last spring and during the summer, but her baby had wandered off and was attacked and killed by a hungry mountain lion. The mother grieved throughout the summer and into the fall, even into her hibernation, and her instincts were still strong. She was aroused by the small animal next to her and wrapped her heavy thick arms around her surrogate cub.

Throughout the night inside the small den, Chauncey struggled to get free but the bear's strength was no match for her.

She was trapped and panicked. She began to cry out.

Callie bolted awake and stood, her nose to the morning air. She moved slowly to the edge of a ridge and froze to a point. Her tail quivered nervously.

Dru woke.

"What is it, girl?"

Callie barked.

"What do you smell?"

She had picked up Chauncey's scent. But it was mixed with another smell, a rank odor, something foreign. She knew her friend was in danger.

She turned to Dru and barked frantically.

Dru packed their few belongings and fixed her snowshoes.

"Find, Callie, find!" she commanded.

They ran into the forest.

They were miles from Chauncey and it would take them most of the day to reach her, possibly into the night.

Chauncey's continued shifting and crying was upsetting the mother bear and she tightened her grip. Chauncey struggled mightily to break free, whining desperately, pleading for her release.

She knew had to keep quiet and let the bear relax if she had any chance, but even in sleep, the giant's hairy arms had locked her in a tremendous vice and, in the small space, it was impossible for her to move.

She had been trapped in the den for ten hours now.

Callie was locked onto Chauncey's scent. Dru ran behind her despite her fatigue. She knew they were not near any towns and she wasn't even sure how far they had come or even how long they had been in the woods now.

By that afternoon, they stopped on a ridge overlooking a wooded valley. Dru looked at her dog. The normally athletic Callie panted wildly and looked weak. She wasn't sure how much further they could travel.

Dru scanned the distant tree-covered hills. It was quiet and seemed peaceful but an undercurrent of fear ran through her. Chauncey might be injured or sick. Even trapped. They rested on an overlook into a valley.

Thirty minutes passed. Callie jumped up and cocked her head.

"What, girl?"

Dru rose and leaned forward. She heard nothing. But Callie's tail was quivering wildly. She let out a short yelp and looked back.

Dru stepped forward onto the rock and cupped her hands.

"Chauncey! Chauncey!" Her voice echoed across the valley.

Silence.

Then, she heard a far-off weak bark. It was shrill and uncertain, but still, a bark. Then a second, stronger than the first. She yelled again.

"CHAUNCEY!"

Then, below them in the valley, she heard a distinct muffled yelp.

Dru pointed down the hill and commanded Callie.

"Get her girl…go get her!"

Callie, now energized, leapt off the ridge and pounded down the hill through the melting slush, barking, crying out for her companion. She disappeared into the woods.

Dru untied her snowshoes and lunged down the hill after her dog sliding on the melting snow and mud. It took over twenty minutes to reach the cries.

At the bottom of the valley, Callie stood on an embankment, pointing away from Dru, her tail shaking wildly.

Dru reached her dog and crouched down but couldn't see anything. Callie's nose was pointed at a large snow mound with a dark opening.

Dru pushed her head next to Callie and cupped her eyes.

Then she saw Chauncey. Her small face peered out from an enormous bed of black fur. Her eyes were filled with great fear.

She couldn't make out what was embedded around her.

In her excitement at seeing Dru, Chauncey squirmed to get loose.

Then, the immense head of a black bear rose, its small dark eyes reflecting the light in a ghost-like glow. But the bear was unable to focus on the immediate disturbance in front of her yet it smelled the threat. Dru pulled back and grabbed Callie, who was struggling to get at Chauncey.

Dru wasn't going to let the beast take her girl. She pushed her head into the opening and bared her teeth at the bear's face.

"Get away from her you *bitch*!"

She wound up and threw her arm into the opening, punching the bear's arm violently.

The animal wrinkled its muzzle and let out a nasty growl.

She knew the mother wasn't going to let Chauncey free.

The bear's arm shot out of the opening at her, its huge claw catching Dru's jacket and throwing her to the ground.

But the bear's arm was now free, and Chauncey had an advantage.

She pulled her hind leg up and kicked against the bear's other arm, catapulting her free and out of its grip. With one sweeping motion, Chauncey tumbled through the opening of the den, rolling out to Dru's side.

Callie jumped to the den, barking wildly at the bear's face inches away.

The animal's head pushed out of the den, growing ferociously at the treats before her as she pushed violently against the den's opening, but her fat body couldn't get through.

Callie wasn't having any of this. Her considerable speed and determination outmatched the sluggish mother and she dove in inches from the bear's face and erupted in deafening barks that blew decisively into the ursine's face.

The bear pulled back, giving Dru the advantage. She grabbed a heavy branch and slammed it against the bear's arm.

The sudden insult incensed the creature. It swiped the branch, flinging it into the forest like a small twig. The bear was now in full attack mode. It pushed mightily against the opening, which began to widen and break open.

Still halfway outside its den, the bear swung its arms wildly about, bellowing at the threats before it. The bear's bite was the force of a sledge hammer with razor teeth and she was ready to eliminate the treats before her.

But the dogs had other ideas. Years earlier, they had stopped a large wolf in these very forests. They were older now and not as fast, but their intelligence and training outmatched the primordial creature.

Chauncey and Callie carefully circled about the half-exposed animal, closing in on either side of it from the mound. The bear suddenly lost its focus, looking to her right, then left, up and back to her right. The dogs could see the shift in the creature's eyes as she twisted nervously from side to side, trying to land a strike. Callie and Chauncey jumped about the bear, this way, then that, in rapid, almost choreographed moves. They moved inches from the creature's face, their powerful barks erupting on both sides of the confused animal.

The mother cried out, awkwardly contorting about.

The dogs' strength had commanded her.

Defeated, the bear bellowed a low grumbling response and pulled back into its warm den.

Dru collapsed in the snow. Both dogs were at her, crying in excitement and freedom. She grabbed Chauncey's face and looked at her.

"Oh my God, girl…where have you been?"

Chauncey licked her face in joy and sprang to Callie, her flanks heaving wildly, joyfully, at her hard-fought freedom.

The two dogs danced about each other like triumphant woodland creatures.

They were together again!

26

The hospital conference room was silent except for papers shuffling between doctors. Brigid sat across the table from them, trying to read their thoughts.

Dr. Davis looked up at her.

"Your sister has been through a lot in the past two weeks, Miss Murphy. She's stable but we're treating her to reduce the heart damage. She'll need rehabilitation before she can return home, but even then, you'll have to stay with her to manage any side effects from the medications."

Brigid stared at a long two-page list of instructions. The paper began to shake.

"Is she going to make it?"

"We don't know how she'll react to the medications. She'll need to be transferred to our long-term care facility first. The Farber Regional Cardiac Center in Chesterboro, Mass. It's our closest facility to her home in Glenriver."

"Long term? I live near East Cabot and work there. It'll require adjustments. I'll have to find a way to do this…."

Brigid looked down, trying to compose herself.

"You'll need to go through training to learn how to manage her care if she does return home."

"If? Doctor, this doesn't sound positive. I don't understand how my sister could have gone from the healthy woman I saw just a week ago to this. I've been in her room while she sleeps. She keeps calling names and has nightmares, crying in her sleep. I don't know what it means. Is there something I need to know?"

"She's experienced trauma to her heart. We think this may resolve in time," Dr. Davis said.

The question was obviously avoided. The doctors looked at each other in preparation to leave.

"Please sign these release forms and we can get Shannon up to Chesterboro by ambulance. You can follow her and make sure she gets settled in. She should be ready by tomorrow afternoon. It's a three-hour drive.

The two doctors left the room, leaving Brigid with the cardiac care nurse.

"Do you know why my sister seems so confused? We've been together our whole lives. I've never seen her so sad and distant."

"Brigid, many times, patients who experience a major trauma like your sister become disoriented and confused, even sad."

"It seems like something else, nurse. She cries out for something while she's asleep. I don't think it's a dream. It seems real. Her mental state seems frail."

"Her rehabilitation at the Farber Center will help with that. It will include visits from a psychologist that can help her."

"Psychologist? What good will that do if they don't know what's troubling her?"

"They are trained to find out. The facility is one of our best. We have many patients there who have gone through similar circumstances as your sister and do very well."

But Brigid knew her sister's condition wasn't positive. The doctors had told her that without resolution of the loss, patients with broken heart syndrome can suffer months, even years after the event, some never recovering.

Brigid knew she wasn't going to get answers. She'd have to guide her sister back to health on her own. Shannon was family, her only family and she would do anything for her.

It had taken two exhausting days trudging through snows and mud with little food. They arrived back at the homestead late afternoon.

This was the first time Chauncey had been back at her old home since Dirck had died a year earlier.

They were famished and Dru emptied the refrigerator of the remaining cheese and vegetables and left to get food at Winger's.

Mabel recognized Dru as she walked through the market door.

"Hello ma'am. Ever find tha' dog a-yours?"

"Yes, we did! I just found her in the woods south of here. She's back safely now. We're out of food and haven't eaten much in two days."

Mabel abruptly went to the back of the store and returned with a large premade hoagie sandwich.

"Enjoy. On me."

She devoured half of the fat grinder.

"'Yep. Tha' woman was in hereah. Tha' one livin' up there at the Judge Benson place."

"Shannon?"

"Yep. Nice woman, middle-aged gal."

"Yes, that's her. When was this?"

"Well, let's see. Was 'bout a week ago...can't quite rememba'."

"By any chance, did she see the poster you put up for our missing dog, Chauncey?"

"Oh surely! I pulled it off and showed it to her. She didn't take that news too well. Got upset quick like. Especially when I told her that the dog had been lost before and may not make it this time."

"Oh God! You told her that?"

"Somethin' like that. She got powerful upset and began to cry. Saw her sittin' out there in the parkin' lot for a while, upset."

"That's what probably caused her heart…."

"Heart? Did she have a heart problem? Is she okay then?"

Dru didn't answer. She began loading her cart with bags of dog food and groceries.

"I'll buy this and be on my way."

"Sorry, didn't mean to bother you, ma'am."

"It's okay. I've got two hungry dogs at home. Have to go."

It was dark when she returned home. The lights were off and the dogs were at the door, wagging their tails. She ripped open a bag of 'Pedigree' beef kibble and poured huge helpings into two large bowls with warm water. The dogs dove into the food, spilling pellets onto the kitchen floor. They both collapsed in front of their empty bowls.

Dru wasn't hungry after the encounter at Winger's. The news Mabel had delivered must have initiated Shannon's heart attack. She had to reach her in Boston her and her know about Chauncey.

She dialed Dr. Davis's number.

"Please enter your pager number," an automated voice said.

She dialed 99022 and rapid beeps sounded and hung up.

In two minutes, her phone rang.

"Dr. Davis's exchange."

"Hello, this is Dru Vaughn, I need to talk to Dr. Davis. He called me about one of his patients, Shannon Murphy. I need to speak with him immediately."

"He's not available now. May I take a message?"

"Need to reach him about his patient, Miss Murphy," she repeated.

"I'm sorry, Miss Vaughn. I handle Dr. Davis's affairs. He's in surgery this evening."

"Can you please have him call me? We need to locate his patient…this is important. She needs the dog we found!"

"Dog? I'm afraid I don't what you're talking about. And the patient you speak of, Shannon Murphy, is no longer here in our facility."

"Isn't there? Has she been sent somewhere else? Where is she?"

"We cannot divulge patient information, Miss Vaughn."

Dru couldn't believe this. She stared blankly out the window.

"Can you please tell Dr. Davis that I called and tell him we have the dog, Chauncey. It's urgent! We have the dog!"

"Thank you. I will let him know you called."

"Please tell him that…."

The call had ended. The hospital receptionist didn't believe the woman and didn't relay her message to Chris Davis.

She immediately punched in Dave Ballard's number.

"Dave…we have her!"

"Thank God! I drove up there yesterday but there was no sign of you or Callie. We saw the snowshoe and dog tracks leading off. I figured you went out on your own after her."

"I couldn't wait. We barely got her…she was trapped in a bear den with an angry mother bear!"

"What? Where was this?"

"Not sure, somewhere damned deep in the woods a lot of miles from here. Dogs saved me. They are my heroes forever. Took us days to get back. Poor girls are dead. Been asleep for hours."

"What about Shannon? Did you find her?"

"The hospital said she has been sent somewhere else but I can't find out where."

"We have to find her!"

"I have a call into her doctor."

"How is Chauncey? Does she look okay?"

"She's thin and exhausted, but I'll take care of that. We'll need to spend at least a couple days up here recuperating before heading back to CAS. And I can use the rest."

"Ok, let me get ahold of the organizers and call off the search. They must have had nearly two hundred folks looking for her."

Dru ended the call and built a fire in the great room. She collapsed onto the couch and downed a much-needed beer as the dogs slept in the kitchen.

Around 1 a.m., she was startled awake by muffled barking upstairs. She ran into the bedroom. Chauncey was standing in the dark room facing the bed.

"Oh, girl. You're back in your old home. You can tell Shannon's been here. You can smell her, can't you?"

Chauncey looked up at her, lost. She knelt and hugged the shivering dog.

"Oh, my girl. You're home now and now you sense Dirck, don't you?"

Chauncey stood and raced past her back down the stairs to the back door, pawing at it frantically. Dru opened the door and she ran to the far field to snowy spot where Shannon had last fallen.

She lay on the spot looking up at Dru.

"I'll help you find her, girl. If it's the last thing I do, I will find Shannon for you!"

Chauncey lay on the snow, her nose pointed to the ground. It was as if she had to face the loss of Dirck all over again on returning home, the only home she had ever known, the place she had devoted herself to her master.

But now, there was nothing left, only the fading scent buried beneath her in the snow.

27

Spring had arrived in the north country after an unusually harsh and pale winter. The damp earth birthed welcoming frons of young ferns, trillium and daffodils, of pussy willows and fields of chartreuse grasses, brightening slumped spirits.

Activity at CAS was bustling. New puppies were in training, service dogs were working towards their pairings with veterans, and therapy dogs were readied for their assignments in hospitals.

Over the winter months, Chauncey had few therapy visits, only twice to a facility that had requested the "Golden Angel." Dru had spent the winter at CAS with the dejected dog, hiking with her around the facility, mostly just laying low. She knew that Chauncey would never be the same carefree and sweet Golden she had known in the first eight years of her life.

Chauncey was now nine and her face had turned white, the jet-black nose had faded and was edged with pink, and the brilliant sparking eyes had faded. But her spirit reined and the frequent long outings in the snow and now the warming spring fields kept her character intact. And as the winter had come to an end, Chauncey's heightened sense of smell had also receded. The memories it had brought, too, seemed to have been dulled into simple disconnected threads of recollections that, in the end, gave her much-needed peace. She seemed to enjoy was just in front of her nose. And while Dru could see she was less troubled, it still saddened her to see her favorite dog retreat into such a simple existence. Chauncey's unbounded enthusiasm, that unbreakable spirit and devotion she once had with Dirck, remained in Dru's memory, and some nights, she'd stare into the white face of the sleeping dog beside her and silently cry herself to sleep.

By mid-May, new therapy requests arrived at CAS, some asking for Chauncey. Dave covered many of the requests with Callie and two other therapy dogs in service. Dru wanted easier visits for her dog, just to keep her skills sharp but not to overburden her with the more highly stressful encounters, which sometimes could leave dogs depressed and anxious for days.

One new assignment caught her eye.

It was for a young girl, Abbie, who had undergone surgery to remove a large brain tumor, leaving the ten-year-old in a wheelchair. The girl hadn't smiled or spoken to anyone in months after the surgery, and Dru felt such a child would be a perfect match for Chauncey who was especially good at lifting the spirits of younger patients. It would be just like Jessie, the young girl with cancer that Chauncey had first met.

She made arrangements for the following week to visit the Massachusetts facility.

The morning they left, it was one of those dazzling Vermont May days. In every direction, the rolling hills were awash with soft verdant greens punctuated by bright pink and white apple blossoms and lavender tulips. The air was filled with freshly mown grass. Dru fastened her harness to the front seatbelt so Chauncey could enjoy the view. During the two-hour trip from CAS, Chauncey watched the trees fly by, her nose pointed to the half-open window as she sampled the sweet spring wind, reminding her of her first trip to Vermont on the day Dirck had brought her to her new home.

They arrived at the facility at noon, an hour before their one o'clock appointment. This was a town Dru had never seen before.

She wanted Chauncey relaxed before her appointment and they walked along the one-block main street.

"Such a beautiful baby," said an older woman as she stopped before them. "May I pet?"

"Yes, she'd love that."

The woman uneasily bent down and placed her hands on Chauncey's face and slowly stroked her muzzle.

"I lost my sweet boy just this past winter. His name was "Jeffery," a black Newfie. I miss him so."

"I'm glad you got to meet Chauncey. She's a therapy dog and we're here to meet a patient in your local facility."

"Oh, yes, that's a good place. We're lucky to have that facility."

"Are all the patients local?"

"Oh no, some of them come from far way away to get here. It's tops in the field."

The woman stared into Chauncey's eyes.

"Your girl looks smart. Chauncey is a perfect name for her. But something seems to trouble her so."

"Yes, she's had a difficult time this past year. She was a service dog to a veteran who passed away."

"Oh dear, that would be a shock. Jeffery was my comfort dog. They are godsends, especially us older folks."

"Yes, I know how important they are. I trained Chauncey at my facility in New York. Canine Assisting Soldiers. Here's my card if you want to consider a companion dog."

The woman examined the card and looked at Chauncey.

"You train these dogs? Bless you for that. Your girl Chauncey looks like she connects with the sick and disabled. I can tell she's sensitive. It's in her eyes, just the way she's looking at me right now. A sensitive soul."

"You're very perceptive. She's extraordinarily sensitive and has made a wonderful therapy dog. But she's been through a lot. These therapy sessions help her from going too much inside of herself."

"I can see that. But she looks like she's searching for something."

Dru stared at the woman and cocked her head. The old woman's face was wrinkled and her blue eyes had faded, but wisdom beamed from her.

"What do you mean?"

"This dog's soul is wanting something, something important that she's been searching for. I don't know what that is, but she's not complete without it."

Dru straightened up.

"You're right. A big part of her was ripped away when her handler died. And she's searching for that."

"She'll find it...find it soon," the woman said as she stared into Chauncey's eyes.

"I hope you're right."

She slowly stood to leave but Chauncey didn't move. She was staring up at the old woman, looking to her for something. She knelt back to the dog and put her face against her forehead.

"Be strong, young girl. You'll find it. You will. You're a good girl, you are."

Chauncey lowered her head and buried it into the woman's arm. Dru couldn't believe this. She rarely acted like this with strangers.

She tugged on the leash.

"Okay, girl. It's time. We need to go meet our young patient."

She led her away but as the old woman walked off, Chauncey turned back and watched as she disappeared around the corner.

"You liked her, didn't you, girl?"

Chauncey looked at Dru and smiled.

They drove to the facility at the edge of town. The campus was spread over three acres with several buildings. She was instructed to visit Building 2A, one of several one-story brick buildings. Something about the place made her uneasy.

Chauncey wore her bright orange vest emblazoned in white with **THERAPY DOG**. They walked into the lobby.

A young woman behind a large desk stood and smiled.

"You must be Dru. And this is Chauncey?"

Chauncey's tail whipped about as the woman approached her.

"Oh, she's so beautiful. May I?"

"Only briefly. I need to keep her focused. Once she's inside a facility, she knows it's time to work."

"Oh yes, I'm sorry. Let's go into the conference room and go over your meeting with Abbie."

They sat next to each other in the large room, Chauncey lying quietly at their feet gazing about the room. She knew this was a work place.

"Abbie Langly is a ten-year-old girl who had a tumor removed from her brain six months ago. It left her unable to walk and she's been confined to a wheelchair since the surgery. Doctors think she might regain the use of her legs but that's uncertain. She can't speak but can see and hear fine. The experience has left her depressed and that's what we're dealing with here. We believe connecting her with a therapy dog would help draw Abbie away from the dark place she's in. Her parents Neddie and James will be there for support. It's been extraordinarily difficult for them over the past months, but they're willing to do anything to help her daughter. Here's some photos of her."

They showed Abbie in her happier times. Running, playing, smiling, laughing at the camera, in constant motion. The last photo had been taken a week ago. She was in a wheelchair. The young girl's eyes were downcast and dull. Her color was gone. She looked older, almost like a sick adult. But through the girl's sad face, Dru could still see the child's spirit still there and knew Chauncey could bring it out. She looked down at her dog.

"I think Chauncey will be able to help Abbie. Her sensitivity with sick children is well-known."

"Wonderful. Abbie is in the pediatric wing in Building 5B. It's a short walk up there. They are expecting you. I'll show the way."

The sunny day was warm, in the sixties, and the walk to Building 5B was pleasant. As they approached the entrance, Chauncey hesitated and stopped, staring at another building off to her left. She barked. Dru looked about but there were no people and they were far from any traffic. She knelt to her.

"What is it girl? You don't know these buildings, do you? It will be okay. You'll find your way."

Chauncey seemed to relax but as she approached the front door, she looked again to her left and nervously sniffed the air.

They walked into the lobby and their escort led them down a long hall to the room. The door was open.

"Here we are. Hello everyone."

At the entrance to the room, a young girl sat motionless in her wheelchair. She appeared small, engulfed in the large mechanical chair. Since her operation, her blonde hair had been kept short and was spiked in wildly different directions with pink coloring and she wore a bright orange jumpsuit with green and red dogs printed on it. The effect was funny and sad at the same time.

The girl looked down and didn't move.

The nurse stepped forward.

"Dru, we're so happy to see you. I know Abbie has been looking forward to meeting Chauncey."

But of course, the nurse wouldn't have known that. From the looks of the young child, Dru knew her dog's work was going to be difficult.

The nurse leaned over the wheelchair.

"Abbie, honey. We have a nice dog for you to meet. She loves little girls and she wants to especially meet you."

Dru led Chauncey to the girl and knelt. She removed her lead. The girl didn't move.

"Chauncey wants to say hello, Abbie," Dru said as she stared up into the girl's vacant eyes.

Chauncey looked up at the girl's face. She immediately knew something was wrong with the child and she could smell sorrow and fear in the room. Her gaze remained on the girl. After a silent minute, she sat, pulled her head back and panted, her black lips curling towards her ears.

The dog's smile registered. Abbie looked up and reached her hand to Chauncey's head. A weak smile drew across the girl's face.

Dru stepped back and signaled to the parents and nurse not to move. The moment was theirs.

Chauncey licked the girl's small hand. The tactile sense of her tongue stimulated Abbie and she leaned forward. She knew the girl wanted more and moved up to lick her face. Abbie jumped back in delighted silence.

She smiled at the dog before her.

Dru moved her arm up and with swift motion, Chauncey caught the edge of the girl's wheelchair and gently rose to her. Abbie pulled back and looked at the gentle dog looming over her but wasn't afraid. Her mouth opened into a silent laugh.

Abbie's mother Neddie buried her face into her husband's arm and wept. They hadn't seen their daughter smile or laugh in weeks.

Chauncey knew she had made the girl feel better and her tail swung freely.

Everyone in the room watched as the pair communicated in silence. The girl now looked like she was giggling, but no sound rose from her. She had two hands on Chauncey's thick ruff, energetically rubbing it, reveling with the dog, laughing in silence. Chauncey began playing with the girl, letting out small yelps and barks, reaching in for another lick, pulling back to again expose her ruff for the girl's delight.

In play, Chauncey leaned to her side towards an opened window.

A breeze blew across her.

She suddenly jumped from the girl's wheelchair and backed away, moving about nervously.

Dru knelt to her.

"Chauncy…what is it? Are we done girl?"

She let out a nervous bark. Dru tried to understand the change in her dog but there was no time to react.

Chauncey turned and ran through the door and down the hallway. Dru raced after her but she was too far to catch. She watched as her dog scurried down the corridor, knocking through nurses wheeling carts, their bottles flying. She headed for the front door, bursting through a family with a young boy. The front-desk nurse raced after the panicked dog but couldn't catch her before she already well out in the courtyard.

Dru raced down the hallway after her. Behind her, she heard the loud voice of a young girl.

"CHAUNCEY! COME BACK!"

It was Abbie. The girl was calling for the dog that had given the child her voice back.

But there was no time to go back.

She ran out to the courtyard and caught Chauncey running in the distance towards another building.

"Chauncey!"

She didn't respond.

She saw a man opening the far building's door. Chauncey bolted past him inside.

It took Dru seconds to reach the lobby. A nurse stood at the front desk, pointing down a corridor.

Dru ran down the hallway.

At the end of a long passageway was a lone room with an open door. Inside sat a woman slumped in her wheelchair facing away towards an unmade bed. Her greying hair was matted to one side and the side of her face was pale and drawn. She didn't move.

Chauncey froze in the doorway, her hind legs quivering. In an uncertain moment, she let out a short, high bark.

The sound jolted the woman. She clumsily grabbed one of the wheels and pulled herself about.

Chauncey leaned in, her nose quivering wildly.

Dru didn't recognize the woman. Her face was strained and her eyes were withdrawn and distant.

The woman stared at the dog before her.

Then her eyes widened and she smiled.

Beyond the worn face, Dru recognized that smile.

"My God. It's Shannon," Dru said to herself.

Chauncey walked slowly to the wheelchair and looked up at the woman, her eyes bright, almost pleading at her. Her tail swung lightly, unsure of herself.

Shannon leaned forward.

"Chauncey!" Shannon said.

Her face suddenly flushed red. She smiled broadly.

Chauncey leapt up to the wheelchair and pressed her body against Shannon, rubbing her head into hers.

She lowered herself onto the woman's chest.

Chauncey recognized that heartbeat. It was Dirck Hansen's. She had listened to her master's heart so many times in the past, for it reassured her that he lived and that she was complete.

And now he was again alive. Alive in the woman next to her.

They remained motionless for a long while before Shannon pulled back and wrapped her arms around the shivering dog.

"Oh, Chauncey, I have waited so long for you!"

Chauncey pulled back and looked into Shannon's eyes. The love of Dirck beamed from her.

She jerked wildly about, licking Shannon's face, whining, yelping loudly in delight.

Dru stood in the doorway, watching them. She stepped forward and knelt.

"Shannon, I can't tell you how much we worried about you, where you were, how you were. Chauncey searched so long for you. She never gave up."

But there was no answer.

The woman and her dog were locked in a world of their own.

28

The flush of spring had receded, ushering forth the warm and welcome winds of summer that rolled softly over the Vermont hills, filling gardens with pink teacup roses and sweet lavender echinacea. It was the top of the live-long year, motionless and silent in breathless days with its blank white dawns and glaring noons, and sunsets smeared with too much color.

The story ended where it had begun, here at Judge Benson's homestead, the place Chauncey had shared with her master Dirck Hansen. Now, her life would continue with Shannon Murphy. Dru had signed over to Shannon the deed to the homestead and with it, Chauncey. She belonged here with Shannon, who carried Dirck's spirit with the great love of this remarkable dog.

Less than a week after Chauncey had found her, Shannon had left the Farber Regional Cardiac Center in Chesterboro, Massachusetts. She had been at the facility for nearly six months and had deteriorated to the point that the medical team had advised Brigid she would likely never return home. She was not expected to live more than another year, yet it had taken only days for her to stand from her wheelchair and walk from the facility, full of life and hope. In his thirty years of treating heart patients, Christopher Davis had never seen such a dramatic turnaround.

In the end, it revealed the power of love to restore the heart, to gather faith and supreme determination. Faith between a devoted dog and her first love.

Dru and Callie had stayed behind with Shannon that week along with Brigid who was spending the summer with her sister.

The day after Shannon returned to the homestead, Dru had revealed the great truth. They had gone upstairs to the bedroom that overlooked the property, as it was the most intimate setting Dru could imagine. At the foot of the bed, they sat close to one other in chairs underneath the large window.

Chauncey lay before them looking up her two favorite women.

"Shannon, I need to tell you something that will put your life into perspective and remove the doubts and fears you have faced over the past year."

"Yes, Dru. What is it?"

"Your heart, the heart you received, the heart that gave you back life, also brought life to this home and to the dog before you."

Shannon cocked her head.

"You received Dirck Hansen's heart, Shannon. He was an organ donor and his heart was transplanted into you."

Shannon's eyes fluttered and she felt faint. She grabbed the edge of the chair.

She looked down at Chauncey.

"My God! That's why I had those battle nightmares, the visions, the dreams of dogs, the soldier talking to me. It explains the panic I felt when I heard Chauncey was gone. That's what made my heart break. It's from Dirck that I feel the love for this homestead and landscape, our neighbors. And now the love I feel for Chauncey. It's indescribable."

She reached for Dru's hand.

"I know now how Dirck felt, Dru. How he loved, and still loves this place, and especially his dog. I can feel it."

She looked at Dru through blinding tears.

"Dirck lives in me. He's so happy I have Chauncey. I feel honored that I am now her guardian, to keep her safe and happy through the remainder of her life."

Chauncey's tail thumped the floor and smiled up at them.

"It's a privilege to have you as her master, Shannon. You must know how much I loved Dirck. We had gone through so much together. He was part of my family. There are stories that you will hear, stories of the journey that Dirck and Chauncey had taken these past many years. They are together heartbreaking and glorious and only make the bond you have with this wonderful girl so meaningful."

Shannon knelt and put her arms around Chauncey.

"I will cherish her forever, Dru. Forever."

Chauncey licked her face. They both laughed.

"We can talk more later. Tomorrow's your big day and we need to start preparing."

The next day was the twentieth of July, and a large midsummer gathering was underway at the homestead, a gathering celebrating Shannon Murphy's life.

By noon that next day, over sixty people filled the homestead grounds. There were twelve dogs, some of them service and therapy dogs brought by Dave Ballard and the CAS trainers. Many of the volunteers who had spent weeks searching for Chauncey were in attendance. Drs. Chris Davis and Patricia Tatters from the Dana Farber drove up for the gathering. There were the neighbors Jake and Joannie Tollinger and their dog Barney, and her neighbor Sarah Bristoll, who, that day, had walked over her own stone wall, just because it was Shannon's special day.

Mabel from Winger's attended as did Gerald Jilly and his wife Mildred from Jilly's store in East Cabot, and Glenriver's historian, Mr. Poindexter. Even Bud Travis, Caledonian's editor drove up to see Shannon. Dru also arranged for the wounded veteran Brig Taylor to be driven up from the Goshen VA to see Chauncey again.

People and dogs spilled onto the wide-spreading expanse enveloped by the graceful interlacing boughs of the weeping willows under the day's imperishable summer-blue sky that seemed to sweep endlessly over the fields like a canopy stretched tightly across the summer-lush landscape.

In the midst of the gathering, Dru caught her dog running towards a car that had just pulled in the driveway. An old man was easing himself from his driver's seat but Chauncey had reached him before he was able to stand. She was whining, her expressive tail swinging at the man as he bent to greet her.

"Good afternoon, Sir. Do I know you? I'm Dru Vaughn."

The man was leaning forward, his head against the dog. He looked up at Dru.

"Not rightly, ma'am. I am Malcolm Longridge from Johnson county south of here. I was told Chauncey lived here. Been thinking about her for some months since she disappeared. Heard about your celebration here."

"Oh, how do you know our girl?"

"She was with me for a while. Saved her from wolves after she was tangled in the woods early last winter. She was a goner for sure before I got to her. I live down that a-way. Brought the sweet dog to my place for some time."

"Wolves? My God, what happened?"

Malcolm Longridge remained in his seat holding onto Chauncey as he recounted the story of how he had saved her, how she had escaped into the forest one day in the big snowstorm, how much he loved the dog. Just like his Jasper.

But he embellished it more than he should have, just to hold onto Chauncey longer.

"We'll Mr. Longridge, you're most welcome here and we're so glad you came. This is Chauncey's home—her keeper is over there.

"Oh yes, Shannon Murphy. Heard her story down at Mac's store. Was on the local news, too. How she received Dirck Hansen's heart. Knew about Dirck and his service dog a long while ago and that he lived here in Judge Benson's old place. Lost my own dog, Jasper, some years ago. Tough without a companion at my age."

"Please join us. We're having a celebration of Shannon's life and she'll be most anxious to hear your story."

Malcom walked unsteadily towards the patio, Chauncey trotting in step with the old man, staring up at him, smiling that beautiful smile of hers. Dru knew that Chauncey understood her life had been saved by the man's hands.

She introduced Malcolm to Shannon and the group and his tale was recounted, this time with a crowd surrounding the man who was rightly given the center seat, Chauncey by his side.

Dru and Dave stood back from the crowd as they watched the animated man waving his arms as he recounted the rescue from wolves.

It was just another part of Chauncey's remarkable history.

"Dave, just look at Chauncey. She looks just like she did when she was first here at the homestead—happy and bright, her spirit restored."

"In all my years of training with you, she's the most remarkable dog I can remember."

"She's touched so many people's lives. I think about Jake Tollinger and his daughter Joannie over there. The man had sought out Dirck those many years ago to admit he has stolen the dog for his daughter, and even through her dark captivity with Jake, Chauncey still held love for him. Then, there's Brig Taylor at the Goshen VA.

Her spirit lifted his so, just like Dirck. I watched them today playing in the field. Brig's walking on his artificial legs now. Chauncey gave him that courage. And now, Malcolm Longridge. In just the few days she had been with him, it had made such a difference in his life. I'm going to get one of our dogs to go home with him."

"And now, she's saved Shannon."

"Especially think of the difference she's made in the children and elderly in the hospitals. Her spirit is so pure and strong. And she did that through the toughest part of her life, without Dirck. Just think what she'll be able to do now."

Chauncey would go on to visit Abbie Langly, the girl that now could speak, and who would eventually regain the use of her legs because of the dog that had given her courage. Chauncey continued her visits to Evan, the boy with pancreatic cancer who had survived and had more appointments with the teenage conjoined twins after they had been separated.

And she got in one last visit with Mrs. Terrance, the ninety-three-year-old widow, before the woman peacefully passed away.

Chauncey changed the course of many people's lives.

Dru would go on to train Shannon to continue Chauncey's therapy work. Despite Bud's insistence that she come back to the *Caledonian Record*, this would now become her life's mission. To help the sick and dying, to give hope to those who had lost it and, like herself, to those who had lost heart in life.

By eight that evening, the sun had set across the Glenriver town line and most of the people and dogs were departing. Dru and Brigid stood outside, shaking the few remaining hands.

Shannon had taken Chauncey inside to the great room as they hadn't been alone all day.

She sat on the leather couch and motioned her dog up.

They were finally alone and the quiet evening settled over them. It was cool in the big room, and the din of the crowd had now faded. From the large bay window, soft purple and blue shadows flickered across the wall like a faded movie of a remembered story.

Chauncey sat close to Shannon, looking at her face, her beautiful eyes. There was a strength and beauty in that face that she hadn't yet discovered but she wanted to discover it all.

But in that moment, a shadow drew across her vision. It was the image of a dark and rainy day, that day not so long ago, the afternoon Dirck Hansen had left her world as she lay in his arms.

It was here, on this very spot, and she remembered well his raspy voice whispering to her:

I need you to know…in my heart…I always will be with you. I make you this promise. Always.

The shadow lifted and Shannon's face was again bright and clear. Chauncey stared into the woman's bright eyes that had thickly gathered with tears. This was her master now, the woman who would guide her through the rest of her life.

Chauncey lowered her head onto Shannon's chest. In the stillness of the quiet room, she listened closely.

The promised heart beat strongly and steadily.

She was finally home.

PROMISED HEART

A novel by
Christopher Dant

The author of **RESCUE**

Christopher Dant is a career writer and studied English and science at Indiana University. From 2000-2004, he attended Stanford University's Creative Writing Program and in 2001, published a collection of short stories *Appalachian Waltz*. In 2018, he published his first novel, *Rescue*. Christopher lives in Vermont with his wife Maureen and Golden Retriever, also named *Chauncey*.

You can find PROMISED HEART on Amazon, Barnes and Noble, or at the Northshire Bookstore at www.northshire.com.

If you enjoyed PROMISED HEART, please consider leaving a review on Amazon.

CPSIA information can be obtained
at www.ICGtesting.com
Printed in the USA
LVHW081349250720
661522LV00014B/954

9 781605 715018